the unfinished world

amber sparks

the unfinished world

and other stories

LIVERIGHT PUBLISHING CORPORATION

A Division of W. W. Norton & Company

Independent Publishers Since 1923

New York • London

Publication Credits

The Janitor in Space (*American Fiction*); The Lizzie Borden Jazz Babies (*The Collagist*); The Logic of the Loaded Heart (*Composite Arts Magazine*); Take Your Daughter to the Slaughter (*Stymie*); Thirteen Ways of Destroying a Painting (*Gigantic Worlds*); And the World Was Crowded with Things That Meant Love (*Matter Press*); Birds with Teeth (*The Collagist*); Things You Should Know About Cassandra Dee (*Atticus Review*); The Fires of Western Heaven (*Barrelhouse*); The Process of Human Decay (*Shut Up/Look Pretty* anthology); For These Humans Who Cannot Fly (*HTMLGIANT*); The Men and Women Like Him (*Guernica*); We Were Holy Once (*Granta*)

For information about permission to reproduce selections from this book, write to Permissions, Liveright Publishing Corporation, a division of W. W. Norton & Company, Inc., 500 Fifth Avenue, New York, NY 10110

For information about special discounts for bulk purchases, please contact W. W. Norton Special Sales at specialsales@wwnorton.com or 800-233-4830

Manufacturing by RR Donnelley
Book design by Dana Sloan
Production manager: Lauren Abbate

Library of Congress Cataloging-in-Publication Data

Names: Sparks, Amber.
Title: The unfinished world : and other stories / Amber Sparks.
Description: First edition. | New York : Liveright Publishing Corporation, a division of W. W. Norton & Company, [2016]
Identifiers: LCCN 2015035414 | ISBN 9781631490903 (softcover)
Classification: LCC PS3619.P3474 A6 2016 | DDC 813/.6—dc23 LC record available at http://lccn.loc.gov/2015035414

ISBN 978-1-63149-090-3 (pbk)

Liveright Publishing Corporation
500 Fifth Avenue, New York, N.Y. 10110
www.wwnorton.com

W. W. Norton & Company Ltd.
Castle House, 75/76 Wells Street, London W1T 3QT

1 2 3 4 5 6 7 8 9 0

For Isadora

May you grow into every hero, defeat every villain, and show kindness to every misunderstood monster.

Contents

CONTENTS

Come, my friends,

'Tis not too late to seek a newer world.

Push off, and sitting well in order smite

The sounding furrows; for my purpose holds

To sail beyond the sunset, and the baths

Of all the western stars, until I die.

It may be that the gulfs will wash us down:

It may be we shall touch the Happy Isles,

And see the great Achilles, whom we knew.

Tho' much is taken, much abides; and tho'

We are not now that strength which in old days

Moved earth and heaven; that which we are, we are;

One equal temper of heroic hearts,

Made weak by time and fate, but strong in will

To strive, to seek, to find, and not to yield.

—ALFRED, LORD TENNYSON, FROM "ULYSSES"

A man is a god in ruins.

—RALPH WALDO EMERSON

the unfinished world

The Janitor in Space

The janitor makes her way through the corridor with purpose, suctioning space dust and human debris from crevices of the space station. She is good at her job. She can push off from the walls in a steady trajectory without even looking; her eyes are always on the windows and the impossibly bright stars beyond.

The astronauts are good, but unclean, thinks the space janitor. Like the astronaut who left liquid salt floating in little globs all over the kitchen today. Like the lady astronauts who leave bloody tampons unsecured and spill bits of powder into the air. Like the male astronauts who leave their dirty underwear drifting around their cabin modules, their worn-through tube socks smelling of cheese and old syrup. And the dead skin flakes—so many flakes she wonders how any skin could be left to wrap all that muscle and bone. Of course she rarely sees the astronauts, so while she assumes they still have skin, it is possible they have shed their skin entirely, that they have, like strange insects, exchanged their soft outside layers for hard, black, shining exoskeletons instead.

She almost never sees anyone except the night watchman, an

elderly mute who spends most of the night watching porn in the security office. She never complains about his unsavory habits, though. She wouldn't even know who to complain to. She supposes the astronauts watch porn, anyway. Or maybe not; good people don't watch such things, she remembers from her time on Earth.

The janitor knows that being good is not the same as being clean. She, for instance, is very clean, but she is not very good. She is still traveling on her way toward that. She told her pastor that she was coming up here to be closer to God, but really she just wanted to get away from Earth. She was tired of waiting to be recognized, waiting for someone to hear her name and turn, eyes too big, full of questions and dangerous curiosity.

People will think you're prideful, wanting to go up in space, her only friend had said. He worked in the state-owned liquor store where she bought a case of Miller Lite every Tuesday morning, after her shift at the hospital ended. She always worked nights; fewer waking bodies around, less human chaos. She never much liked talking, and after the close crowds of the jail, she liked to be far from the hum and buzz.

The space station staff liked her when they interviewed her—she seemed polite and quiet and incurious. That was important. One of the astronauts, a bearded Russian with kind eyes, asked her a question: Will you be lonely in space? She looked at the faint lines scrawled around his eyes and forehead, and she supposed he had a family somewhere, maybe small children. Yes, she said, but I have always been lonely. The astronaut nodded, and she could see he understood. She could see his aquiline profile as he turned to someone offscreen, and she knew she would get the job.

The astronauts occasionally get up during the night, and then the janitor tries to be a shadow, a gray bird. She ducks out of sight, floats to the ceiling in rooms where they wander, terrified they will appear different during the artificial night of space; sure she, too, will be different. Sure that starlight will strip away the years, will fall upon a thirteen-year-old girl alone on a dirt road, a bruise on her face and the mop clenched painfully in her broken fist. The things, the nightmare things fear could claim you for. The dark hurts in the veins, the heart-deep hurts in the buried parts of the body. The faces that chase her, even now, even in the farthest fields of space where nothing grows, nothing whispers, nothing lives or dies but the first things that ever got made in the universe. She isn't sure whether she believes in God or not, though she always told her pastor she did. She isn't sure any woman ought to believe in God.

In lockup, most of the women didn't. They said the name of God and the name of certain men and spat, teeth pressed together in a kind of crooked, inward anger. She learned to push a mop and broom in prison, learned to be useful. It was a good thing to be of some use in this world. Or, she revised, in this universe. It was hard sometimes, to get used to this new way of thinking, to bobbling round the Earth like a second moon. She felt free, free of all the accumulated debris of a lifetime in sin and sacrifice, free of the burden of people for the first time in her whole flat life. She felt small and bright and diamond-hard, a little star in the firmament.

The light was so bright here, always, despite the darkness of the spaces in between. The fluorescents scattered throughout the station, the milky white light of the nebulae. The twinkling reds and greens and yellows of the instrument panels. The soft blue glow of the Earth over her shoulder. It was comforting, like a street on Earth at Christmastime: a sleepy rainbow glow over these travelers straying so far from home.

Light of my life, he sang to her while he had her on his knee. She was just a baby, broad-faced and raw. And if nobody ever loved you, it was easy for somebody to tell you such pretty things. It was easy for you to sit by while they did such unpretty things. She suctions up drops of urine and thinks about how it felt to hold a gun, how that boy and girl never even looked at her face while she held it. She dropped it like a snake; it felt like a dishonest thing, something so solid but, really, a dirty hollow pair of barrels. He laughed at her and picked it up, like he was made to hold it. His hands slid all over that steel and wood just like they did all over her.

She scrubs the fingerprints from the instrument panels, watches the lights flicker and dim. She wonders how many rags she'll go through, how many surfaces have to get clean before she can finally empty herself of the past. She doesn't know about metaphors but she knows that even the smallest human vessel has boundless storage for sorrow. Was there a right way to take in so much sorrow it burned clean through the lungs and heart? Was there a right way to atone?

There is, she thinks, a kind of atonement in hard, honest work. And so each night she suctions, sweeps, mops, waxes, shakes out rugs, cleans and stocks the bathrooms, launders and changes the bedding, collects and disposes of trash, replaces lights, polishes the smooth metal, and washes the walls and ceilings. She cleans lint, dust, oil, and grease from their machines, cleans the glassware and lab equipment, soaps down sinks and sterilizes microscopes. She refills and labels tubes and bottles in her careful, neat handwriting. She keeps the station clean and shiny as the future.

She feels at home beyond the skies. She lied and said she came here to be close to God, but she feels further away from Him than ever. God was everywhere in the fields and farms of her childhood; God was on everybody's lips and in their books and on their walls. God was the fire and the twisted face and the crippled-up preacher.

God rose from the steam off the fields, crystallized in the oil puddles at the service station, was the cold stones in the neighbor's pond after his boy died of polio. God was the iron lung around those family farms, squeezing, squeezing, and everybody dying inside.

She feels happiest near the deep green shadows pooled in the corners of the station, listening to the low hum against the endless silence of the stars. This feels safer than God. It feels honest. It feels removed from any human notion of heaven.

One night, she is scrubbing at a smudge on a window when the bearded Russian comes floating around the corner, pajama bottoms trailing and sleep-crusted eyes nearly shut. She pushes up, clings to the ceiling, breath held. But the Russian doesn't even look her way; he glides past her to the wide wall of windows and puts his face to the glass like a child. *Gde vy,* he murmurs, and she doesn't know what the words mean, but she understands. The pastor once said death was the gift of a wise god—and she wondered whether he really believed that. To her death seems the opposite of wisdom, the opposite of mystery, the opposite of being out here in this vast wondrous place. Death is the opposite of lonely, and lonely is the only thing the janitor owns. It is the only thing that's hers. And that makes loneliness beautiful, out here among the cold and bright beginnings.

The Lizzie Borden Jazz Babies

One month before the jazz babies were born, their father sacrificed himself on the altar of the god Mammon; that is to say, he finally overworked himself into a heart attack in the accounting offices of the J&J Department Stores Incorporated. The jazz babies' mother never liked to talk about it. Mention of the incident gave her a tremendous attack of nerves, accompanied by a terrific headache. Ever since the father's death (and probably before), she had become the sort of person who avoided telephone calls and rung doorbells in case they preceded bad news.

One day before the jazz babies were born, Sergei Diaghilev's Ballets Russes was dancing the premiere performance of *The Rite of Spring* at the Théâtre des Champs-Élysées. This was across the Atlantic, it's true, but the babies' mother swore the ripples from the cataclysmic concert rocketed her into early labor and doomed her twins to a life of aggressively modern behavior and a love of dangerous music.

One hour before the jazz babies were born, Al Jolson was recording "You Made Me Love You," for wax cylinder, a song the twins' mother would sing to them often in the next year, while dreaming of the menswear salesman with whom she went dancing on Saturdays (after a respectable period of mourning). Fifteen years later, the jazz babies (so-called, self-named) are over the moon about Al Jolson tying the knot with Ruby Keeler. The twins have a dance act, and both hope they look like Ruby while soft-shoeing it on the front porch of their mother's and the menswear salesman's new bungalow.

The twins are blond with big heads, skinny bodies dangling below like strings under balloons. They are that mysterious age, not nymphets but not quite children; the age when awkward figures leave open the question of what they will develop into in a few short years. They lack grace but have a kind of buoyancy. It worries their mother, as does everything else under the sun, from animal attacks to the Oriental influence to modern bathing costumes.

It has been in all the papers, the menswear salesman tells the mother. Grown women wearing bathing costumes in the middle of the park, the palazzo, the promenade; gathering en masse in bathing costumes and eating pizza. Lips smacking, thighs jiggling, arm fat flapping—the salesman shudders and stops, unable to go on. The jazz babies' mother does not own a bathing suit, and in church the next Sunday she prays, in her nervous, insincere way, for the souls of the sinners that do. She also prays for her first husband in heaven, for the neighbors' yappy dog to drop dead, and for a new wireless set.

The jazz babies' parents forbid them to continue their dancing on the porch. Once it was adorable, a sweet novelty to watch the two little girls, indistinguishable but for a small splotch of birthmark on the left heel of the eldest twin, hoofing it to the sounds of Hoagy Carmichael, Fats Waller, and Jelly Roll Morton. Their big finish had always been "Hard-Hearted Hannah (The Vamp of Savannah)," though the only reason they got away with it was that their mother, unfamiliar with Theda Bara, thought the lyrics were about chastity.

Now, however, they are attracting a different kind of crowd: leering men, drawn to the gangly girls' early puberty and no longer quite innocent hip flares and flashes of skin. They went from the Charleston to the Black Bottom to the Lindy Hop—this last one, with its obscene shimmies and twists, giving their mother and the menswear salesman fits. Now when they shake what god gave them while Dolly Kay belts out "She's a gal who loves to see men suffer," the whole scene takes on a distinctly unwholesome tone. Grown men begin hanging around the bungalow after dark, watching the girls catch fireflies. They follow the girls to school, offer to carry their books, make marriage proposals behind hedges. It is as if these men—most of them well past forty and fathers themselves—can sense a sort of dormant, smoldering sexuality and want to be first on the scene when it bursts into full bloom. After the babies' mother catches two men climbing through the bathroom window to wait for the inevitable, she quickly and hysterically puts a stop to the whole thing.

No more Lindy Hop, no more jazz, she tells them. No more vulgar public displays. If you want to dance you can take ballet lessons like every other nice little girl.

We're not nice little girls, says jazz baby number one. Her name is Patience, but everyone calls her Patty. She's the twin with the birthmark, just a minute older than her sibling.

That's right, Mother, says jazz baby number two. Her name is Charity, but everybody calls her Cat. She, born second, always agrees with her elder sibling. We aren't nice and we aren't little girls, either.

I don't care what you are, says the menswear salesman, I'm not having the pair of you prancing around like showgirls. I paid for this place by the sweat of my brow and by god, I won't have you girls turning it into a house of sin. The menswear salesman, like many middle-class men of his age, is always talking about his house: the work he's done on his house, how much he paid for his house, and the sweat and tears and blood that flooded the purchase and upkeep of his house. The twins like to mock these bourgeois concerns. They are bright girls, emerging razor sharp through the fuzzy haze of puberty, and not the sort to forgive sentimentality. They are hard-hearted Hannahs, Cat and Patty. They are emblems of this new age, tricksters unable to be tricked. And as they go into temporary retreat after the belt and the broom are threatened, they start making plans to kill their parents.

They change their imaginary stage name, from the Blue Falls County Jazz Babies to the Lizzie Borden Jazz Babies. They wonder how much an ax weighs and if they are strong enough to wield one. Separately? Together? They draw detailed pictures and check out all the books about Lizzie they can find in the library. They discuss ways to blame a killing on intruders. They discuss ways they could charm the police. They play their records on the gramophone, over and over, and dance the Lindy in the sad solitude of their bungalow bedroom. *"To tease them and thrill them, to torture and kill them, is her delight, they say . . ."* They study hard and get good grades, to deflect suspicion. They take ballet lessons.

Then Cat, Cat the second, Cat the accomplice, starts dating a boy. He is a nice, clunky-looking thing, half-formed in that way most young men are, and he is sixteen and strong and Cat thinks he is beautiful. He stops by the house to court her, and the menswear salesman likes the creases in his trousers. No bad young man, he tells his wife, would wear such sharp creases. Besides, his father is a wealthy farmer in the next town over, and they own a brand-new mahogany-colored Model Q. The menswear salesman approves of modern consumerism, if not modern music.

Patty approves of none of this. For the first time in their whole lives, she refuses to speak to Cat. She feels like driftwood, like something dragging along—a useless appendage. She feels betrayed. Cat cries all night, offers to introduce her to the young man's cousin. She begs her twin to speak to her again. Patty slips her a note: "GET RID OF HIM." Cat cries again, but refuses. She believes she is in love. She believes that, for the first time, her heart is kindling, her body a brightening blaze. For the first time, her fingers and toes are no longer numb, her heart no longer frozen in the confusion of youth. Her heart is a little oyster shell, opening, opening.

Patty, meanwhile, continues to make plans. But she no longer shares them with her sister. Every day after school she heads to the library, where it is assumed she is studying diligently, but where she is really researching the Borden murders. She wishes her family were wealthy so there would be a maid to blame. She wishes she were just a little bit bigger; there is no way for her to swing an ax alone, and anyhow, her mother and the menswear salesman do not own an ax. She makes lists of poisons, and how to attain them. She saves her pocket money. She is, though she refuses to believe it, desperately lonely for the first time in her life. She has not yet decided if she will poison her sister, too.

Somehow the twins begin to grow, quite literally, apart. It is as though the rift between them has taken on a physicality, a kind of separation that finds itself in form as well as function. Cat continues with ballet and remains buoyant, floats long and lean, while Patty takes up tennis and becomes muscular and compact, all her grace anchored firmly in the earth. Cat is lovely and serious; Patty is sensual, all smiles and come-hither stares. She steps out with men older than the menswear salesman. She goes to wild parties, takes up smoking, hems her skirts above her knees, hides racy novels under the mattress. Cat reads Molière and dreams of marriage with the wealthy farm boy. She has never had to carry a conversation; that was Patty's job. She feels, always, at a loss for words. She is sometimes content, but often she thinks she may drift away entirely, so unmoored she has become by the loss of her sister. Patty feels cleaved, still lonely, but liberated. She learns how to work a previously underutilized dimple on her left cheek, and fine-tunes the tones of innuendo in her pretty, deepening voice. She becomes popular. She decides to become an actress, though she does not tell her mother and the menswear salesman, who have definite opinions of women who "go onto the stage."

The jazz babies still listen to jazz but are no longer an act, no longer a pair. They still share a room but Patty has strung a bedsheet across the middle of it, halving it neatly, and they do not cross into each other's spaces. Patty keeps her pearls and poison lists and Gershwin records stockpiled in a locked drawer, and Cat has no idea her sister still has nefarious notions. Cat keeps her toe shoes and Fats Waller records in plain sight. Neither sister knows where Hard-Hearted Hannah has gone. It seems somehow to be the part of the sisters that disappeared in the split.

One night, Patty comes home very drunk from a party and passes out on the divan. The menswear salesman and their mother are due back any moment from bridge club, and Cat does not know what to do. She looks at the clock, at the door, at her sister's face, sweet and young in such sleep, even under the rouge and the lipstick and the jeweled headband. She dithers and waits—she has not touched her sister in months, not a kiss or a hug or a caress—but finally she hoists Patty by the armpits and half-walks, half-drags her to their bedroom. She is surprised by her twin's weight—when did Patty get so solid? But they finally make it, and Patty is laid out on the bed, and Cat removes her boots and stockings, her dress and girdle, as gently as a lover would. Patty snores like an old woman. When she is laid out, fully bare, Cat stares at this new body, no longer a mirror of her own. They have different muscles now, different thin and fat places, different soft and hard places. Cat pulls the covers up to her sister's chin and kisses her forehead. Patty's eyes pop open, just for a moment, flicker into consciousness. I think, she says to Cat—the first words she has spoken in six months to her twin—I think I will let you live.

Later that night, when Cat is tucked in her own bed and dreaming of riding in the wealthy farm boy's Model Q, her sister suddenly intrudes. In the dream, they are driving around a sharp corner, and Patty appears just around the bend, planted in the middle of the pavement. They stop the car and realize, too late, that Patty is holding an ax behind her back. She swings, and swings, until the farm boy is a bloody blur on the road, and then she turns to Cat. I think I will let you live, she says, and Cat kneels on the pavement beside the farm boy's remains. She puts her trembling hands over his body, butterflies over flame. His body is so warm still, her own hands warm over the heat of it. Behind her, the car is dead, its arteries grown cold.

The Cemetery for Lost Faces

Louise and Clarence are pinning butterflies to a board. Louise's eyes are wide in appreciation of the markings, orange and gold, but Clarence's are closed. He doesn't want to see the flightless wings. Louise takes his hand and squeezes it, tells him it's okay. The pins don't hurt them, she says. They're dead.

Clarence understands that his older sister is brave and he is not. And even at two years old he adores her. Even at two he knows she is the sky and all the stars scattered over it. He squeezes back. The siblings are beautiful in the light, golden and brown sprites in tattered jeans. Their mother frowns and says to their father, They should be in school, with other children. This is when their mother was still speaking to their father, if only just.

School! Their father laughs. This *is* school. And they're learning what's important, not a lot of nonsense. They're learning how to live in the world.

Are they, their mother says. Or are they learning to leave it?

You would know, says their father, and for just a moment the sun falls out of the sky. The two parents make stone figures, faces turned downward; life-sized gargoyles against the gray. Pain ripples through the space where they stand, frigid air in the lungs and nostrils.

Then suddenly, the sun is back, and the warmth is back, and the blue and brown and gold is back. Their father laughs, and the world is tipped back toward summer once more.

•

It just goes to show, people said later. It just goes to show how fairy tales always stop too soon in the telling.

Others said it was never a fairy tale at all. Anyone could see that. They were all too lovely, too obviously doomed.

But the wisest said, that's exactly what a fairy tale is. The happily-ever-after is just a false front. It hides the hungry darkness inside.

•

The funeral was the first thing they'd ever wanted to forget. Yet with the bodies came the unbidden hoarding of memories, the desire to consume and digest their parents' histories whole. With the bodies came the beginnings of silence, too, though neither of them much minded. Preservation of the past requires a monastic sort of quiet. A hushed pause in dusty rooms.

Before the service Louise found Clarence weeping over their mother's coffin, trying to pry open the lid. They're sealed shut, Clarence, she told him, grasping his hands, pulling them hard. He jerked and shuddered and his face fell into shadow. How can we remember what they looked like? he asked, and the question was acid in Louise's veins.

Clarence and Louise were not children, but they were still

young when their parents drove into a ravine and died. They were still left very much alone.

◆

Clarence is already tall as a man, with small, restless hands. He begs bones and horns from the slaughterhouse, carves things like combs, hairpins, buttons and figurines. Louise sits beside him in their playroom, stretching scraps of hide over plaster-of-Paris frames.

Clarence and Louise are trapping death in amber. They are learning how to make time stop.

◆

Home has always been less house than sideshow gallery, a careless museum of strange objects and curiosities, filled to the brim with cheap knickknacks and sentimental turn-of-the-century souvenirs by the hoarding habits of their great-great-grandfather and his wife.

There is a room full of sea battle dioramas, another jammed with full-size decorative staircases to nowhere. There are halls lined with ceramic dolls and jelly jars, hurdy-gurdies and Chinese puzzle boxes, tiny ivory elephants and jeweled fans. The ballroom contains a life-sized mechanical music hall orchestra that still wheezes out "It's a Long Way to Tipperary" when you put a quarter in the slot. And the parlor is given over to the display of Victorian taxidermy tableaux. Bird-weddings and classrooms full of kittens, frogs jumping rope—the kind of extreme anthropomorphism in which the Victorians excelled. (Louise and Clarence's great-great-uncle was a taxidermist, famous for his depictions of Beatrix Pot-

17

ter's stories. Their father took up the family calling as well, though he was not in the business of animating picture books. He specialized in mounting trophies for wealthy big-game hunters and museums.)

When she was very young, perhaps four or five, Louise had been given one of the valuable antique taxidermy pieces for her very own. Her father brought it down soberly from the attic and placed it on the mantel above her hearth. It was a tableau of the story of Thumbelina, in rough chronological order, and showed Thumbelina emerging from the flower; Thumbelina, asleep in her walnut-shell cradle, carried off by the toad and her son; Thumbelina being rescued by the fish and the butterfly; Thumbelina on the swallow's back; Thumbelina and the flower-fairy prince at the wedding, butterflies and finches dancing attendance.

Small Louise had been fascinated by the tableau, the animals caught in strange, unnatural poses. She did not care for fairy tales, but she was caught by the lifelike appearance of the creatures and wondered how her great-great-uncle had managed to achieve such a feat. Every day she would study the tiny feathers, the jet beads carefully glued in for eyes, the delicate feet and fins. She studied, Louise, and when she learned to sketch, the Thumbelina creatures were the first thing she drew.

Clarence hated the tableau. Clarence was too softhearted to stand the sight of these long-dead creatures, kept in a mockery of life, their own feathers and fur a double prison. But that was Clarence for you. Louise was made, as her father said, of sterner stuff.

~

Today is the day that Tony comes with the money. His driver and the other man—Jackson, Louise thinks he is called—stay in the big truck but through the window she can see a small black handgun resting on Jackson's lap. The truck has made deep furrows in the road, still soft and wet from the rain yesterday.

Tony is pacing in front of the house now, waiting for the delivery. Waiting for Clarence. He looks up, sees her at the window, waves. He knows she will be watching because she always is. She does not wave back. She never waves back. She does not like Tony, and not because she's afraid of him. Not exactly. He thinks he is fearsome. She has nicknamed him Tony the Tiger and he thinks it's a compliment.

She watches Clarence head over to the carriage house, emerge with the enormous crate on a dolly. She watches him exchange the crate for Tony's cash, watches Tony the Tiger's flashing smile as he heaves the crate into the truck bed, watches the debris the wheels kick up as they slash through the mud and sludge.

❖

Louise at fourteen: quiet, moon-faced, skinny white limbs with prominent veins running through them. Big nose, big eyes, small mouth, pushing long hair out of her face as she helps Father brush the fur of a Siberian tiger.

Father at forty: garrulous, charming, handsome, and mustachioed, dancing through a series of professional and personal failures. He lectures his daughter on the tiger's mating habits, explains how important it is that they respect this creature, teach others to respect it. That is what we do, Louise, he tells her, and his eyes are merry and brown and his fingers are light and small as those of the ladies who make lace in the historical village. He, too, is making something lovely: life, complex and grave and astounding.

Not alive, he tells Louise, he is always telling Louise. We cannot strive for them to look like life.

Then what? she asks, puzzled. Her eyes are perfect mirrors of his. What should they look like?

Like a dream, her father says proudly, for he thinks of himself as a maker of dreams. The dream of a tiger, the dream of a rhino, the dream of a squirrel. The perfect form that preceded all the real tigers and rhinos and squirrels.

Louise at fourteen, shy before such brilliance, asks her father if there is a perfect form for everything in the dream. Even me? she asks.

Louise at thirty-four cannot remember now what answer her father made her, no matter how she opens her brain and shakes out the contents like an overstuffed handbag. Louise at thirty-four cannot remember.

◆

It costs an enormous amount of money to keep up the estate, even without servants. There's the lawn service to pay, the estate taxes, the plumbing company because these old pipes are forever breaking, the roofers because this old roof is forever leaking, and a thousand other costs besides.

And of course, there are the property taxes. Those, finally, prompted Louise to accept the offer from a friend of a friend: to meet privately with a very famous installation artist. Noel needed a discreet, talented taxidermist. His previous taxidermist had just died, No, not that sad, dear, he was good lord nearly a hundred so don't worry about that, but we need a new and brilliant one now, don't we? Noel speaks often in the royal "we," though his bizarre

Brooklyn/posh London mash of an accent sounds more like a bad imitation of both.

She has always considered herself an artist, anyway, and she doesn't like the limelight, so this arrangement suits them both perfectly. Noel pays her well, she pays the property taxes, and she can continue doing exactly what she likes and allowing Clarence to do the same.

And she likes Noel. They are alike, very much alike, except that he is commercially minded and she is not. He is passionate about Audubon and says frankly if he were a better painter he would probably not be so bloody famous. He lost his little boy to brain cancer and his first wife left him six months later. Louise and he have sex sometimes on the floor of her workshop, surrounded by dead teeth and dead skin and the strong smell of formaldehyde. It's not really a fetish so much as it is a pact of sadness, a shared wish to sail through the underworld and rescue the ones who left them long ago.

◆

Louise is a scientist. She is experimenting with new things, working toward a greater knowledge of the world, a vague sort of natural philosopher in her way.

Clarence is an archivist. He collects and makes and organizes to preserve the past. He is working toward an understanding of the world through the memories it already holds.

Brother and sister look nothing alike. A full five years separates them, but no one would blame you for mistaking their unusual, unspoken closeness for the bond between twins.

The space between her and Clarence is a world. Sometimes she thinks they are the sun and moon, each rising when the other dies, each dependent on the other's careful sleep. Together, she thinks, they are two strange creatures, and yet it is only together that they keep this place in a tense stasis; they are the precarious balance by which the estate holds steady.

Clarence at fifteen tries to be brave, just the once. He takes instruction from Louise, and he is, at first, an excellent pupil. His sculptor's hands have always learned to wing their way through solid substance, and at first, soft rabbit skin is much easier to carve than clay.

But then he vomits into the bucket where the guts go, runs from the room, lays his hot face against the pillow and weeps. For himself? For the hare? Louise does not know. She knows she should go to him, but she is her father in so many ways and when she cannot fill a space with words, she will not fill it at all. She cannot help but scorn his softness.

❧

Louise is working on a blue finch when Clarence enters the room, hands gray as a corpse's with packed-in clay. Are you having any luck? he asks politely. He knows she hates doing birds-in-flight. She can never get the feathers to lie as they should.

Louise sighs and puts her brush down gently. Smoke, she says, and pulls out a pack of cigarettes. She packs them and peels open the top, slides one out and slips it between her lips in a graceful way Clarence always admires. He wonders, sometimes aloud and sometimes not, why his pretty, interesting sister has never married. She just smiles enigmatically in a way meant to discomfit him, meant to grab him by the apron strings and tie him tight to the fluttering strips of heart she still has left.

Clarence, she asks, cigarette dangling, when is Tony coming next?

Thursday, he says. He's dropping off another dog for the Big Man.

Louise laughs. Do we have to call him the Big Man, just because Tony does?

I don't know his real name, says Clarence. Don't even know what he looks like. Big Man is fine with me. I met his wife, though. She came up with Tony last time. She's a rhinestone. Must be half his age. He smiles, a soft, happy smile.

Louise doesn't like that smile.

Their working theory is Russian mafia, but really they have no idea who the Big Man is. He found Louise, and he's brought in a few hunting trophies and paid plenty for them. He also keeps dozens of whippets, and when they die he likes to immortalize them in his vast, unseen mansion.

Be careful, says Louise, and blows smoke in Clarence's face. She leans back and watches it swirl across the air between the two of them, catching and distorting his kind features like a fog. You be careful with the Big Man's things.

—◆—

Louise's father first taught her how to preserve and make dreams of the dead. But before she was allowed to touch an animal for reconstruction she was made to learn the basics: anatomy, sculpting, painting, tanning. She learned the long history of taxidermy, even took the train with her father to the Museum of Natural History in the city, so that he could show her the work of the best artists in the country.

She studied Carl Akeley, William T. Hornaday, Walter Potter

and Edward Hart, Roland Ward and the specimens he preserved for Audubon. She learned how to cast a form, how the life in eyes died so you had to make new ones from glass, how to glue on whiskers, and how to extract and reattach teeth. She even learned the best way to clean a skull, how to breed the kind of bacteria that would eat all the meat right off the bone. She paced the woods with her sketchbook, storing the kinetic movement of bodies in dead ink, in her living hands. She got used to the smell of blood, the smell of guts, the smell of the meat that had to die before the body could live again.

—◆—

Shouting outside. Honking. Tony the Tiger and his crew again. She throws a bed jacket over her slip because she has suddenly remembered something: Clarence is sick today. She normally lets him deal with Tony but she will have to do it herself. Her mouth is a moue shape at the thought.

Now she descends the stairs, bridelike in flimsy white, flashing bits of pale skin shot through with green rivers of blood. She fishes around in her jacket pocket to find the key to the carriage house, where the exhibit is crated up and waiting to go home.

At the door, Tony looks her up and down and laughs. He always laughs at her. She doesn't mind but she minds the gun in the car in Jackson's lap and the way the driver stares like a goat in heat. That's why she usually lets Clarence handle this part of the business. He is so tall and looks threatening, though of course really he's as soft and malleable as clay.

Please pull your car up closer, she shouts to the driver. I can't push the crate that far.

The driver just stares, leans out the window, spits. Resumes staring. Smiles. He has a dark unibrow and broken-off brown teeth.

Animal, she says. Tony laughs, long, loud.

We are all animals. You too, no? He comes closer, stands in her sunlight, makes a dark shadow over her. She starts to back up but he grabs her wrist, pulls hard, touches a finger to her lips. You, for instance. You are bat. You are batshit, yes? He laughs and releases her, and she is suddenly glad Clarence isn't here.

Don't touch me again, she says coldly.

Tony smiles. He is not unattractive, maybe too tanned and leathery but she supposes given his age that's not such a bad thing. Better to be preserved, to be pickled, rather than melt down as slow and soft as candle wax. Better to smile than leer. Her stomach goes rather wrong at the thought of what's behind that smile. Follow me, she says, and she honestly doesn't know whether she'd like him to turn around and go, quickly, or to follow her and then . . . and then. Then what?

I can help you with the crate, he says, suddenly contrite. The Big Man will be so happy to see his friend again.

She is glad to have the help getting the crate onto the dolly. The dog was huge, nearly as tall as she was, not to mention the elaborate scene she'd placed him in. Hunting, perfect butterfly balanced on a flower, stump ringed with tiny ants. The perfect companion for a wealthy gangster. The thing he can't kill.

When the car pulls out of the drive, Louise sighs. Whether in relief or frustration, she doesn't know. Her hands are full of money.

❖

When they were small, Louise and Clarence would put their sleds in the back of the car and drive with their father to a hilly place where the mountains started to rise. Louise watched the earth dash by under her sled, arms around her father, trusting that the ground would eventually come up to meet them. She loved that feeling of flying. She loved how everything seemed to sharpen in that moment; how the sled's shadow seemed inked onto the snow. How the soft edges of the pine trees could cut their cheeks like razors as they flew by. There was something about that moment that seemed to stamp the hardness of nature into everything—not in a cruel way—only in the cleanest, most Darwinian sense. It was the nature of avalanches, of hard, icy snow and buried footpaths. The nature of the wild dream before man.

Louise remembered how Clarence was always frightened of the initial jump. When they shared a sled he would hold her waist so tightly she felt her lungs close a little, her arms tingle, and her vision blacken at the edges. She would often return to this memory after her parents' death. She wondered if there was that same strange sense of euphoria, if the world seemed so perfectly black-and-white in those last several seconds. She wondered if the last thing her father saw was his own shadow, flying impossibly over the snow.

◆

Louise as a child eventually learned all she could from Thumbelina. She then took to the parlor, sketched the stilled bobcat, the snowy owl, the dancing mice with their little legs akimbo. She would sit there for hours with her drawing pad and her pencils, sketching the fine lines of whiskers, the wet-looking noses, the curved claws, the tufts of hair in the ears.

Other children would have been terrified, alone in that great dark room with its heavy wall hangings and wine-colored carpets, surrounded by once-living shapes caught in endless predation. Not Louise. Her mother said she didn't suppose Louise could be frightened by anything, that Louise was the only child she'd seen born without fear. Her mother crossed herself as she said it—it seemed unnatural.

But Louise's father used to smile and nod sagely toward his daughter. I've taught her never to be afraid, he would say, and she isn't.

He needed a child who would remain impartial in the face of accurate observation, for without it, what did we have but the terrors of the imagination? It wasn't that her father had no use for imagination—indeed it was essential to his work, to creating the final spark of life. But he also knew what a terrible dictator imagination could be, given unbridled freedom. He had seen it destroy the outer life of his wife, her whole being focused now on what she could dream in her head and keep for her own, the self a prison: just the woman, her pottery wheel, and her stilled and silent tongue.

❧

Shortly after the funeral, her father's uncle asked Louise for a portrait of her parents. Instead Louise sent a violent, angry sketch, the paper almost torn through in places from her heavy crosshatching. It suggested a car, a vast mechanical wreck. Two shapes were crumpled in a heap of what looked like twisted metal, gears, wheels. Clarence was very unhappy when she folded it crudely and stuffed it in an envelope addressed to the uncle.

Well, she said. He asked for a portrait of the two of them.

Louise, he said gently. She was her father's daughter but she'd inherited her mother's black anger. It burned through her sometimes like a chemical fire, brief and devastating and utterly unstoppable. Clarence had no choice but to watch and wait until his sister had cooled into some new shape, until she emerged from the fire patient and calm and even harder than before.

❖

Their mother was always a beauty, tall and fair and well-made. But the lovely brow concealed a deep hurt, a void where pain replaced love, replaced joy, replaced even sadness. Their mother had been a locked box for years.

But every now and then when even she felt the pull toward other people, it was Clarence whom she sought out, Clarence to whom she gave her love and her talent and her self-sufficient steadiness. Louise belonged to their father; she had the same scientific curiosity, the same dancing-but-dogged mind. She had her father's merry eyes and dark hair. So naturally her mother gravitated toward her own mirror, the pale, delicate Clarence, with his bright hair and great gawky height. He was the only one allowed to use her pottery wheel. He was the only one allowed to kiss her good night. He was the only one allowed to love her.

❖

To create life, one must be a keen observer of faces. A raised eyebrow, a crooked laugh, the width of irises. The lines that snake away from the eyes like tributaries, the shadows of cheekbones slicing backward. The way the mouth holds itself just so.

❖

Louise sleeps, dreams of feathers and wings and wild flight through darkened skies. Someone is singing. She sees a flock of pigeons overheard and she remembers something about a town square and December 2nd. Then she wakes, head on the pillow buried in down and feeling wrecked and confused.

Oh. Noel's pigeons. Noel's exhibit is opening in a few months and he needs pigeons. He needs a hundred of them, some installation in a public square. He's hoping he'll be arrested. She needs to get the eyes right, those terrible pink eyes, slick and toxic as rainbows in an oil spill. She's been putting these off because she hates pigeons. She hates to work with something she hates. But Noel does pay her. So she must become again the impartial scientist, immune to any human notion of what is beautiful. She must make a dream of the homeliest birds.

❧

The adults at the funeral watched the young teenagers holding on to one another's hands and were glad to be anything but them, despite their youth and beauty and brilliance. There was something waiting to go rotten in them, everyone could see it in the tableau they made. Everyone could see the future would be difficult to find.

But brother and sister found the past instead. They've kept the memory of their parents alive. In the sightless visages of animal corpses, in the slick wet surface of clay, they create memories of their parents. Gargoyles with their father's grin and their mother's long gaze. Monkeys and cats and turtles with their father's broad nose and their mother's way of tilting her head back just a little, as if to take in more of the world. Clarence works his clay on the wheel, digs his thumbs into the earth, while Louise preserves skin, stretches it over new bones, molds the clay eye sockets and paints the details of claw, of tooth, of pupil and iris. Everywhere the faces of their own creators. Every day they are burying their parents;

they have created a forever cemetery for those lost and broken faces.

❖

At Noel's for dinner. Teesa, his wife, parks a pair of lamb chops in front of Louise and Clarence, and Louise finds she can't quite get her teeth through the blackened meat. Teesa is a horrible cook.

Oh, is it hard for you to eat animals, then? asks Teesa. I suppose it must be. I didn't think to ask.

I'm fine, says Louise. I eat meat.

That's so interesting, says Noel's mother. Her name is Mrs. Ralph Mattson. That's how she introduces herself, without herself included. She's always there at dinner but never seems to eat anything; Louise watches in fascination as she breaks her meal down into component parts and packs it away in her sleeves, her wallet, her pockets. Once Louise watched her tuck a slice of ham into her bra. She doesn't know if the old lady is crazy or just repulsed by Teesa's terrible food. That's so interesting, she repeats, uncertainty flitting over her features. She spears a lamb chop with her fork and opens her pocketbook.

Long silence, broken only by the staccato bursts of forks and knives scraping ceramic. Finally Clarence puts his fork down, says, That gallery that you recommended said no.

Noel swigs wine, shakes his head. Sorry, Clarence. We tried, but he wasn't sure he was interested in pottery. Guess he wasn't.

Not my pottery, anyway, says Clarence mildly.

Noel protests, but Louise is not surprised. Clarence has been working on a new series, modeled after the urns the ancient Egyptians used to store the vital organs of their dead after embalmment. Except that Clarence's urns are made of the vital organs themselves. Louise's favorite is an urn sculpted to look like a bloody, hollowed-out heart, aorta and superior vena cava sitting atop the lid like gloves for alien hands. They have not been popular with Clarence's usual gallerists, who want something pretty they can sell to the tourists. The tourists don't want to drink tea from a teapot that looks like a lung.

We'll keep asking around, says Noel. Those pieces are so brilliant. We know a friend who's working on some project involving ritual—maybe you two could do something together? Clarence shrugs. He's never made art for anyone else. He just does things to see if he can do them. And when he finds he can, he stops and does something else.

Teesa pours out coffee, burnt as the lamb chops. She knows that Noel and Louise are having an affair, but claims not to mind. She prides herself on being unconventional, so she mentions it frequently, with an air of studied boredom. Teesa is one of those people who substitute scarves for personality. Now she dances back to her chair, and watches Louise put down her knife and fork. Oh, she says, I'm always so impressed with your table manners, you and Clarence.

She is forever saying things like this to Louise and Clarence, as if they were feral cats skulking about a farmhouse. As if they were not quite civilized. Louise wants to bite Teesa's thin freckled arms in revenge. Instead she says, quite politely, Oh, we're not exactly Grey Gardens up at the estate, you know. We have running water. We even bathe sometimes.

Noel yelps, his way of laughing. Mrs. Ralph Mattson finishes putting away the last of her food and taps Louise's arm. My dear, the old woman says, gumming the words through thick red lipstick caked over her lips, a bloody cave of bad dentures. That nightmare mouth tells Louise she'd like her little dog to be preserved when he goes. I do think it will be any day now, she says, clicking her tongue.

I can do that, says Louise. Would you like him to be playing? Hunting? Sleeping?

I think mounting a nice-looking bitch, Mrs. Ralph Mattson says cheerfully, and Clarence starts coughing. He looks at Louise, who shrugs, so he continues to drink his coffee with the sort of ferocious delicacy he uses whenever he encounters anything carnal. Louise has never known, of course, if that extends to his affairs, and she does not care to ask.

❦

Louise has been loyal only—almost only—to her brother and father in love. This is not to say she has been a virgin; she has always been open and in fact almost generous in matters of the skin. But in matters of the heart she has been lured but once, long ago. She fell in love with a complexion, pale and soft as ivory silk, lips ripe and rosy, too pretty, almost, to be a man's face at all. And yet there was nothing at all soft about him. His mind had strong legs and his eyes were hard and gray. The beautiful lips shaped determined phrases, anger often braided into the words.

His name was Morris, and he was a pianist, yet another man who relied on his own two hands. She met him during her tour of Europe, the only traveling outside of the States she'd ever done. He was seated next to her at the Vienna Opera House during a performance of *Der Rosenkavalier*. When Octavian gave Sophie the silver rose, Morris reached over, a total stranger, and draped his long, long fingers casually over her upper thigh. She saw him again in front of Mozart's house, and he took her to his hotel and had her on the floor of the tiny tiled bathroom. His fingers played her as expertly as a piano and she responded with fervor to each staccato note, each long sustain.

She failed to finish her tour and instead followed him home to Indiana, where he taught at a university. It lasted for six months but in the end he was too sure of himself and too angry to feel sure of anyone else. He accused her of unspeakable and untrue things. And then on a dark night, flat as the surrounding fields, he took a bottle of pills and died on the living room rug. His wrecked, ghostly face in death was the ugliest thing she'd ever seen. She fled that night, got on a bus and went back home to Clarence. Clarence, who after no word from her for months met her at the door with silence and a glass of bourbon. Clarence, who never asked where she had been.

❖

Clarence has a lover's soul. That's what their father always said, but he understood it to be a weakness.

Clarence disagreed. It's the one thing that makes me really brave: love. It's the poetry of it, I suppose. The nobility. The inevitable tragedy.

Louise had laughed at the time. Tragedy? Clarence's idea of love consisted of one-night stands with the pretty farm girls who worked at Denny's during the winter. What was so noble about that? Human urges, that was all.

Clarence would laugh, too. As close as they were, he never told Louise his most terrible secret: he desperately wanted a love like Mother and Father. Even if, especially if, it meant the destruction that followed. He knew that Louise's forgiveness would never extend that far.

—

When the car pulls up and Tony gets out, Louise is watching from the upstairs bedroom. Her fingertips itch. She thinks of her father, of how he would tease her about these strange urges, how when she was little her fingers and toes would ache and she would long to fly. Use those restless limbs, he'd tell her, laughing. Shake the energy out of those fingers into this little squirrel. Make it dance like you want to.

She watches Clarence and Tony discussing payment. Ducks, embarrassed, as Tony looks up and sees her dark head aimed toward him. She pulls her hair over her face like a curtain and picks up a paintbrush. She can start working on some pigeon eyes. But her fingers are shaking, unsteady, and after a moment she puts down the paintbrush in disgust. She peeks up through her hair, sees Clarence getting into a heated discussion with the man in the truck with the gun. With Jackson.

This is new. She doesn't like this. She throws on a pair of pants, tucks her slip into them like an awkward, billowing shirt, and gallops down the stairs and through the door. Clarence and Jackson are howling at one another, no, rather, Clarence is howling and the man with the gun is pointing the gun at Clarence.

She throws her body uselessly in front of Clarence's, short enough to protect nothing but his least vital parts. Well, least vital for staying alive. Tony is standing to the side, leaning on the hood of the truck and laughing. Beautiful, Louise, he says. Very touching.

Fuck you, she says. What's going on here? She can feel Clarence shaking behind her, just a little. Jackson smiles, deadly calm. He clicks on the safety, puts the gun back down on his lap.

Nothing so much, he says. You just better tell your brother to be careful who he's fucking, so. He shrugs.

Louise turns to Clarence, looks the wide expanse upward at his face. What's this? Fucking who?

Clarence grabs her arm in a way that is most unlike him. Let's go inside. Let's just go inside.

She shakes his arm off, angry and hurt. Clarence has a secret? From her? He starts to stalk inside, tall and faster than she is, and she loses him in the hallway. What is going ON? she shouts, but he is gone inside his workroom and shutting the door in her face. *In her face.* This is new, too. She bangs on the door for a minute before giving up and heading back outside. She is not afraid of the man with the gun. She wants her money. But the truck is gone, and Jackson is gone, and Tony is gone.

This last is unexpectedly hard. She has no idea why it should be. Tony is a leather goon with a grin, that's all. Why should she want him here? Why should she want him at all? But she knows, with the ache in her fingers and toes, that she does. She wants him like she wanted to fly from the rooftop when she was ten, wants to throw her whole body into that catastrophe until she is utterly exhausted and dried up. She hasn't wanted anyone like this since Morris, and just like Clarence's rejection, she doesn't know what to make of it. The shape of her world is changing, off-kilter and blurred, astigmatic.

❧

Mrs. Ralph Mattson arrives in the morning, her Little Boy Blue wrapped in a blanket and reeking already.

We had to observe the customary period of mourning, she explains. Louise nods and marches off to the freezer with the poor little dog. She calls for Clarence, then remembers about their almost-fight. She thinks she heard the car drive off last night. She wonders if he is having his love affair somewhere.

When she gets back, the old lady is wandering down the hall, examining the ships-in-bottles and sea battle dioramas. She murmurs in awe, suddenly child-eyed. This is always the way it is, here in this house, magical since Louise and Clarence were small. They preserve a world long gone in these long rooms, crowded now with dead objects and memories, long devoid of the softening gaze of cheerful people and their love for one another.

⬧

Once, when she was ten, Louise hated Clarence. Just for a day. She mixed her mother's underglazes in a bucket, hoping for something pretty, and was disappointed when the mixture turned a flat brown. When her mother found out, she locked the door of her studio and wouldn't speak to Louise for a week.

After a few days, Louise complained to Clarence. You deserve the silence, he said. You broke her special paints. I won't speak to you, either.

Louise's heart was a white-tipped, furious squall. She told Clarence this was what had happened to Mother and Father. Mother was full of silence and Father was full of guilt, and the air was so heavy with accusations between them it could never be cleared again. She spilled over with rage, spending it on lamps and tables and chairs, until Doctor Lloyd had to drive out and give her a shot to calm her down. Clarence came to see her that night, shamed and sorrowful.

I'm sorry, he said. I don't want to fight ever again. She held her drug-heavy hand over his golden head like a benediction. She was all too ready to forgive, and she told him she always would be. I will never hurt you with my silence, he said. I will never be like Mother.

He curled into her chest like a comma and let her sleepy strength wash over him, let it give him brave dreams.

❧

The dark is heavy tonight; the stars have disappeared behind a wall of clouds. The air feels thick, like something is waiting to happen. Louise is up late because she is starting to be concerned. She is waiting with her heart hinged open for her brother to come home.

Noel calls, speaking in riddles at midnight. We'd like to create a chimera, he says. Can we do that?

Any impossible life is a chimera, Louise says.

Homer's chimera, says Noel. Part lion, part goat, part snake. Is that impossible life, then? Impossible for you?

Louise considers. She doesn't like the idea. It seems a mangling of nature, red in tooth and claw and refusing to be a sideshow. You know, she says, when explorers brought the first platypus back, scientists cut it apart looking for the stitches. They were sure someone had sewn a duck's bill on.

But couldn't you? asks Noel. Couldn't you make something new if you wanted to? Like being god, yeah?

Like being god, agrees Louise. She doesn't believe in god, but Noel already knows that. That isn't what he really means at all.

She imagines the chimera breathing fire behind the wall of clouds tonight, just beyond her vision. Just beyond what she can understand. She shivers and watches the driveway for any signs of life.

❧

Clarence arrived two weeks early, a birthday surprise for their mother, and there wasn't time to get to the hospital. Doctor Lloyd came to the house and delivered Clarence in their parents' bedroom, while Louise and her father watched terrified from the doorway. It took six hours for her brother to be born.

Louise's father and mother held hands after and smiled, exhausted, but happy because they were still in love. They were so absorbed in each other that Louise was first to hold the screaming Clarence. She stroked his strange, wrinkled skin, covered in dark golden down, and he quieted, raptly absorbing her blurred face.

Looks like he loves his big sister already, said Doctor Lloyd, and Louise looked solemnly up at him.

Of course he does, she said. The doctor felt a strange sadness at that, as if he could read a prophecy, as if he could hear the warning bells, buried in the baby's soft whimpers and in the sister's solemn phrases.

❧

Louise is shaping a black bear's ears when the doorbell rings. She flicks on the security camera monitor, sees a blond young woman, very pretty in a loud, artificial way. She's wearing a tracksuit scattered with sequins and a good bit of hair that isn't her own. Louise considers briefly as she's mixing Bondo and fiberglass resin, but decides not to answer the door. She's never interfered in Clarence's amours before, and she doesn't see now as the time to start. The young woman is crying, thick dark mascara tracking new shadows into the terrain of her lovely young face. Louise reaches up and shuts the monitor off. She picks up her knife, makes a small opening between the skin and the cartilage of the bear's right ear.

The doorbell rings again. And again. And then again. Louise sighs, puts down the knife. She takes the stairs two at a time and throws open the door. He's not here, she explains to the tracksuit. It's pink, she sees, pastel pink as a cartoon stomach.

I know, she says. Louise folds her arms. She stares, and Pink Tracksuit crumples further, sitting on the step and gasping. She is clearly in the throes of some kind of hysteria.

Would you like to come in, says Louise, and it is not a question. She tries to pry the girl up by the armpits but Pink Tracksuit is not having any of it. Her mouth keeps working, glossy lips twisting around sobs and half-syllables that seem to keep getting caught before they can emerge. Look, says Louise, not unkindly, I really don't know where Clarence is. He hasn't been around for days.

They shoot him! The words fly from Pink Tracksuit's face like a strong headwind; the spell is broken. Now the language floods the dam, in Russian, in English, in something halfway both, but in between the sobs and the foreign words a phrase, repeated over and over again until Louise is certain it must be true, and is frozen to the step with the horror of it. They shoot him, she says. They shoot him and he is dead.

—❦—

Clarence and Louise outside in the dark. They are teenagers here, brains and bodies growing faster than they can understand. Their parents are mostly gone, but not yet dead.

Look at that moon, says Louise to Clarence. It's surprised at the world tonight. See how its mouth is hanging open?

The Man in the Moon, Clarence tells her, is made up of terrible catastrophes. Firestorms on the terrain.

Louise and Clarence, doing what they've done since they were small: their backs on the front lawn and eyes stretched toward the stars. It really has got a face, though, Louise says. It's not entirely metaphorical. She sketches on the sky with her finger: mouth, nose, eyes.

But that's my point, says Clarence. The things that caused all that damage, those mouth craters and so on, mostly took place forever ago. Before we were even here.

You're saying, says Louise, that it's so typical of our species to give human features to the sad things in space?

I'm saying the world doesn't need our stories. The world is doing just fine without a plot.

Then why bother making all these stories? Louise asks. Why make art at all?

Clarence shrugs, scratches at a mosquito bite on his shoulder. Because what else are we going to do?

◆

Louise is an arrow. She is a blade. She is a flight through the air and a touchdown in skin. She is a bloody hole and she is endlessly spinning down the black, falling through the void, sounds filtering through a second too late, like a badly dubbed film. Filtering screams and footsteps, scuffling in the drive. A thick and heavy, world-ending thud. She watches the road ringed in black, her brother's shadow flying over. Her eyes are red and dry as desert clay.

◆

A car screeching away down the dusty drive.

Louise standing over the long blond body.

Clarence's eyes, open, clouded as the past. She is already forgetting what they looked like clear.

Why do we have no memories for the things we love? she wonders. But Tony.

Tony the Tiger.

Tony the trophy.

Tony, who has dropped her dead brother in this dirt road with less reverence than one of the Big Man's dogs. Tony, who has proved a thug, a villain, a gangster with her heart flattening in his fist.

Tony the dead body, slumped over the backseat.

Tony's life pooling onto the leather seats. A skinning knife in Tony's heart.

The Big Man will consider it fair, in the end; above all else he understands vengeance. He understands what love burns away, and what it leaves behind.

The Logic of the Loaded Heart

If John is three, and John's mother is six times his age, how old was John's mother when John was conceived in the back of Al Neill's pickup truck after a Styx concert in Milwaukee? If John's parents spend 100 times zero days being actual parents to John, how many days' total is that? Does your answer change if John's mother sometimes bought him Mr Pibb and lottery tickets when she stopped at the gas station on her way home from work?

Extra credit: Please calculate the probability that at his mother's current age, John will drop out of school and work in a burger joint while playing lead guitar in a heavy metal band called The Slaughterhouse Four.

When John is six, his father goes to prison for attempted robbery of the Rocky Rococo Pizza in Delavan, Wisconsin. Please calculate the probability that The Slaughterhouse Four will open for Def Leppard at the Minnesota State Fair in what will be the brightest shining moment and impossible dream of John's life.

At thirty-six, John has three ex-wives, one current wife, and nine children. (Holy shit, John.) If John still works in fast food, and his youthful good looks have sunken like a shipwreck with the passage of time, how many women in this bar will go home with him tonight?

How many women will go home with John tonight if John's band, now called Shards of Death, is playing tonight at this bar? Does that number increase or decrease if John is wearing a T-shirt that says "Swallow or It's Going in Your Eye"?

Amy has had five Amstel Lights, and her blood alcohol level is .08. If John is fifteen years older than Amy, how many hours will it be until she wakes up in his apartment, hungover and horrified by her poor decision-making?

If John's wife comes home from her night shift at Perkins at that precise moment, and her anger level is rising at a rate of 3 millimeters per second, what is the volume of John's wife's anger after the approximately fifteen seconds it takes John to put on his pants?

Extra credit: How many minutes until John's wife threatens to take the kids and the money and leave? How many days until John's wife sneaks into the basement at three in the morning and puts holes through his favorite electric guitar with a long series drill bit?

John hires a man to kill his wife, and agrees to pay him 30 percent up front, and the rest when the job is completed. If the total amount is $100,000, how much will the hired man get up front? And how many years will the judge subtract from or add to John's sentence if he was high on crack cocaine when he ordered the killing?

Bonus question: If John is $11K in debt and agrees to pay a contract killer $100K, how long does John have to live?

John's band has had four names—but not at the same time. The first year, John changes his band's name and then he changes it again at evenly spaced intervals over the course of twelve years. How many years separate each name change, and how many years will the names "Viking Fists" and "Ogres' Blood" cause the judge to add to John's attempted murder sentence? Does it even matter? Will John have a new life in prison? Will it be better, or maybe at least cleaner, tidier, than the one outside?

Bonus extra credit: If John's mother at fifteen and his father at twenty were given extraordinary foresight, would they have fallen in love? Would they have stood in line, in the raw cold and rain, for those Styx tickets? Would they have listened to the nostalgic-yet-aspirational lyrics of "Come Sail Away" and thought, We *could* set an open course for the virgin sea? Would they have climbed into the back of that pickup truck in the afterglow, nails and bolts under bare skin and school and plant shift not withstanding? Would they have purchased extra condoms at the five-and-dime? Would they have wanted to preserve all they had—or would they have taken a chance, anyway, because when love sings down the microphone and strikes you, who can say what would happen if you failed to swoon and fall at its feet? Who can say whether A leads to B leads to C or how many apples John ended up with in the end? Who can say why the loaded heart defies all logic, like an unfinished word problem, like a riddle written in the human dust of a crowded barroom?

Thirteen Ways of Destroying a Painting

O *ne:* The time traveler leaves her craft in a copse of trees near the center of the park. She walks quickly—as quickly as she can these days, with her aging knees and hips. She buys a flimsy little card and takes the subway downtown till she reaches the poorest part of the city. She finds the artist at home amidst the squalor, paints scattered, no hot water, barely room for a dirty mattress. Downstairs a baby cries. He is so young, the artist, a white smooth face in the dark of his walk-up. She supposes this will be easy—from the empty, hungry tilt of his face, to the stooped posture from painting under this sloped attic roof. She tells him her name, the name of a very famous sculptor: a lie. She tells him she has heard rumors, but finds he has no talent, that his paintings are no good: a lie, also. She tells him he should move back home to Modesto, become a dentist. There is money and there is security in dentistry. There is emotional stability and happiness.

The artist looks at her, aghast but defiant. The artist knows his way around this kind of truth.

When the time traveler returns to her own time, she heads

straight to the third gallery on the third floor of the museum. The painting still hangs—a vast, moon-filled abstract, shapes building to a woman, curves like rolling blue hills, lit from within and without. The room is crowded with people who have seen it only on holo screens, breathless in its physical presence. The dates under the artist's name, bookended by the long-ago *b.* and *d.* The painting is now titled *In Spite Of.*

Two: The time traveler counts three, and throws the dummy onto the highway as the bottle-green Ford comes barreling over the bridge. After the smash-up, she calls the young artist collect from a Modesto diner. There's been a terrible accident, she says. Long recovery ahead, come home for good, she says. When she gets back to her present and sees the painting, she isn't exactly surprised. The artist never had much filial feeling.

Three: The time traveler sits at dinner with the artist's muse and the man she has hired to seduce the artist's muse. The muse is pretty, her eyes a soft gray and her hair a bright gold. She is tall and strong, with large breasts and hips, and the man has been happy to do his job. The time traveler buys bottle after bottle of wine for the table, until the man puts his hand on the muse's thigh and her face softens into a sweet smile. The time traveler is no voyeur, but she stands for a long time under the muse's open window, listening to the low moans float onto the warm summer air.

She returns to her own time and the painting still hangs. Now it is titled *Forgiveness.*

Four: The time traveler steals the artist's rent from his dresser drawer. His landlord, she knows, is an unyielding sort. Now the painting is smaller, much smaller, but it is still the single occupant of the room and it still sucks the air from the room and it still lights the room from within and without. Fuck, says the time traveler, and the tourists standing nearest her shift uneasily in polite Midwestern disapproval.

Five: The time traveler posts an acceptance letter from a California dental college, complete with a nine-hundred-dollar bonus if the artist enrolls in the next two weeks. The painting is bigger again, and the bio on the wall mentions, as a humorous bit of trivia, that the artist briefly considered dental school. Can you imagine, it says. The artist as a dentist! The time traveler resents the exclamation point, as do all the dentists who pass through the museum.

Six: The time traveler sets explosive charges under the apartment, and blows them when no one is home. Upon return, the painting is still there, and now a tour guide is lecturing on the painter's subsequent madness. The artist, he says with an air of enlightened detachment, claimed to have created a series of paintings using his own waste—which his wife unfortunately destroyed. The tourists make faces.

Seven: The time traveler sets fire to the unfinished painting. The painting is still there.

Eight: The time traveler pours acid on the unfinished painting. The painting is still there.

Nine: The time traveler paints over the unfinished painting. The painting is still there.

Ten: The time traveler steals the unfinished painting and buries it in the past of the past. The painting is still there.

Eleven: The time traveler curses, cuts, spits on, slashes, saws in half, kicks, pours water over, blowtorches, burns to bits, eats the ashes of, smashes the easel around, throws out the paints for, and washes her hands of the unfinished painting. In triumph, she returns to the museum.

The painting is still there. It hangs, suspended, "like an artfully falling ocean," says a pretentious young gentleman in a straw boater and suspenders. The time traveler thinks of artfully falling anvils instead.

Twelve: The time traveler steals the unfinished painting and takes it back to the future, where it disappears like smoke upon arrival. And the painting is still there, is still there, is still there, *is still there—* is still hanging in the gallery and now it is titled *Perseverance.* The time traveler feels the unfairness of this keenly. She has persevered. She has not succeeded. She has not made him see his own sad end, there in that bedroom with his failures and his guns and his useless, incomprehensible war with the painting. All that genius given, all that misery marked for both of them.

Thirteen: The time traveler finds the muse at her lunch. She watches the muse eat her sandwich with gusto: tomato and cheese on thick slabs of crusty bread. She watches the muse gulp down wine, watches her strong white teeth and her smooth white throat. The time traveler sighs. She was more in love with life than with him— she'd never have believed how black and long the days could stretch over her, mean and empty, like shadows in the winter. She takes out the pill, drops it into the muse's wineglass. She leaves before the gray eyes can close. She still needs them to see, just for a moment until the timeline catches up.

The time traveler materializes in the gallery, where the painting no longer hangs. Now there is another painting, lilies on a pond, and Google finds only a retired dentist in Modesto, California. The time traveler smiles then, a soft, sweet smile, and no, her limbs don't start to fade away, nor does that smile hang on the air, nor does she slowly dissolve, like pixels on a screen or shadows over a wall. She simply smiles, and then isn't.

Lancelot in the Lost Places of the World

Lancelot has been summoned out of sleep to find a secret kingdom. Dreams of daffodil hair and golden summer smoke all drifted away when the earth opened above and the men shoveled him out. You have been to the Perilous Chapel, they said. You can help us find what we seek.

He does not think he has been of much help so far. The expedition is traveling in terrain he is unused to, unfamiliar with, and in his weakened state he can barely hold a sword. The men, strange in their colorful threads and accented voices, are looking for another kind of relic: the lost kingdom of Prester John. The Prester descended from the Magi themselves, it was said; he was the ruler of a fruitful land, full of new plants and animals, of new kinds of people. Nestorians and their descendants, heavy with the riches of their flight from other worlds.

These warriors with whom he travels now are not knights, but they claim a quest just the same. They are seeking this fabled hidden kingdom and all the treasures inside: the Gates of Alexander, the Fountain of Youth itself, and especially, most especially, a wondrous mirror, in which every part of a ruler's land can be seen at a word. It is this mirror their master has sent them for. He is a foreign prince, Lancelot has been made to understand, and he desires the mirror to help him wipe out his enemies. Such men have always sought such artifacts.

They have been traveling in a dark jungle for days. Lancelot does not know jungles; he has never known such uncomfortable and wet heat. The damp reminds him of the damp he and Gwin made when their bodies came together. He misses her bright, brassy smell. He does not like this place. It has too many eyes. The men chatter to themselves and Lancelot cannot understand them and he is shorter than everybody here. And he is bored. There are no devilish knights to joust with, no castles to besiege and break. Only this vague heat and a cascade of invisible threats, surrounding them in the jungle like nightmares waiting to pounce. He is afraid of these nightmares. Defenseless against things he has never seen, he sleeps with his head to the tent, avoiding attack from behind.

The men are taking turns cutting through vines, hacking and slashing and cursing the foliage in this miserable heat and humidity. Mosquitos swarm the party, and the mules stop, well, mulishly in protest, half-hidden behind a lacy veil of pests. One of the beasts has just attempted to shed its pack again, standing firm and four times heavier in the middle of a small copse of trees, when Lancelot feels eyes on the back of his head. The men laugh, thinking he has gone stupid from too much time under the soil. Those are insects, they say, slapping at the backs of their necks and palming the blood smears as if to pantomime. Lancelot rolls his eyes. Even outside of space and time there seems to be a language barrier when it comes to metaphor.

Something is *watching*, he says. Following. I can feel it.

The men are still laughing, but not as hard now, and their eyes narrow as they survey their surroundings. These are not careless men. They have not earned the favor of their prince by being foolish. They fan out to the edges of the path. They wait, laughter fading down into a buzz saw of jungle silence, which is not a silence at all so much as a warning.

Lancelot is not the first to see it, but he is the first to believe it. A pale man, body and hair the color of paper, almost nude but for a leather loincloth and holding a sharp wooden spear. He appears in an instant as though he'd fallen from the sky.

He blinks, slowly. Just the once. Stands extraordinarily still.

We are looking for the kingdom of Prester John, says Lancelot. His heart swims into his throat for his own lost kingdom, but he swallows it down and watches the man's spear carefully, ready to duck or dodge if necessary. The spear lowers, inch by inch, spear hand relaxing. The man's face makes a bitter smile. And bitter, notes Lancelot, translates through all the many languages and races of the world. Bitter has a note that's hard to miss.

We seek the same, says the man, and he gestures. Some thirty-odd men like him, all paper-colored and silent, emerge from the surrounding trees and stand with spears at the ready. The prince's men, normally taciturn and unshakable, shout in surprise. Lancelot cannot understand how the pale men managed to hide themselves among all this dark and greenery. He thinks it is a trick he would very much like to learn.

Would you like to join us? asks Lancelot. We can seek for this kingdom together, and split the treasure among ourselves. The prince's men mutter darkly; Lancelot is offering what he has not been authorized to give. The prince's men begin to wonder if digging up a hero was in fact a mistake. Some of the prince's men had argued for making a golem instead, and it is looking like perhaps they were right after all. But it doesn't matter in the end, because the pale men want nothing to do with the prince's men and their search. At Lancelot's words, they break into a single hiss, like a long white snake, and then fade into fog, into mist, into nothing. Lancelot and the prince's men stand their ground, uneasy for a time. Eventually, as the sun begins to loosen its grip on the blue overhead, they seek for a place to camp. To rest for the night and to water the mules.

They've only made it a short way forward when there comes a wailing like a heart run through.

Everyone turns and stares, watches helpless as the swampy sand opens and eats one of the men and his mule. One by one, small mouths of jungle-earth emerge and drown the prince's men where they stand. The ground rumbles and churns, men and mules shriek and run about, and in the sand's grumbling Lancelot hears the warning: We are the seekers. We will seek those who quest for what is hidden, and we will swallow you whole. We will keep the kingdom safe.

Lancelot does not want to be swallowed here, so far from where his king and queen lay. He smells green in the air, and in wild panic to live seizes a nearby vine and pulls himself up. He is face to face with a tiny monkey, old-man-faced and screeching. Lancelot has never seen a monkey before, but somehow he recognizes a relative. He is encouraged. He suddenly feels he has been *made* to swing from treetops, in the way that heroes do. As the men below dance about, avoiding the sand's hunger, Lancelot flies to another tree, and then another, until finally he spots solid ground below. The remaining men gape as he calls to them, but only for a moment. These may be foreigners but they are not fools. If gravity has suspended her pull for a moment, they will happily follow suit. After the ground has given up the chase, Lancelot waits at a respectful distance while the others mourn their dead and distribute their belongings.

Later that night, they come to the edge of what looks like a village. There is a clearing, and a clump of small huts; a group of tall men in hooded robes confer in hushed tones by torchlight. Their eyes glow like embers, but their faces remain in darkness. As if in a dream, Lancelot opens the door to the nearest hut, drawing his sword. But his weapons would be useless here; he knows this. Another tall man, taller even than the others, stoops by a fireplace, half-hidden and half-flamed by the meager fire in the hearth. He is tossing papers and books to the floor, he is muttering to himself. He is too absorbed in his search to notice Lancelot at first. But then he hears the scuffle of footsteps, turns, looks with no surprise on the knight and the band of men behind him. Where his face should be is a pool of ink, spreading in the soft firelight.

Is this Prester John's kingdom? asks Lancelot.

The man laughs, hateful, bitter. We are also searchers, he says. We have only just arrived ourselves. And we will depart as you will: empty-handed, empty-hearted.

But who are you, Lancelot says. No real question. The answer does not matter. They are seekers, that is all. He suddenly understands that there is no kingdom. There are only the seekers and the lost places they drive toward, always just out of reach.

And with that, he breathes a last breath of stone and copper, of green and damp, of soil and skin. Then he tumbles to bones and is still, sleeping once more, and now the men must find their own way home.

And the World Was Crowded with Things That Meant Love

They met only once, at a piano recital in her hometown. Both of them were there for other people's children. He caught her yawning while a blonde in pigtails murdered *The Blue Danube*, and they exchanged grins. After drinks and dinner they were delighted to find they shared a hobby: both were sculptors of sorts, though she worked in clay and he worked in wood. Both had jobs that sent them round the world, and it was a way to kill the long, late hours that haunt the solitary traveler.

She started the exchanges, the reminders they sent to one another as they aged in different cities, countries, hemispheres. But that would come later. At first it was the dinner, and the drinks, and the porch outside where her laughing relatives lingered. At first it was her childhood bedroom, the quilt flung to the floor, the way she moved like a dancer and the way she flung her arms about and the way he surprised them both by bursting into tears. At first it was finding their faces fit perfectly, a jigsaw. A locket severed and the halves hung round the neck of the world they would cross many times over the years, always looking for one another.

The first piece was a bust, a child's head and shoulders. The pig-tailed pianist. A drawer at the nape of her neck, with a little heart inside. A paper heart, coin-sized and inked in scarlet. He kept it in his pocket until it fell to pieces.

His eventual response: a small wooden copy of *den lille havfrue*, Andersen's little mermaid on her rock. But instead of the sea woman's visage, it was her own features carved into the soft basswood. She smiled when she saw how well he remembered her face.

Down the years they sent their strange missives. She sent maps made of clay, locks with no key, books with words cut out, fantastical animals and landscapes. He sent puzzle boxes, lacquered bangles engraved with *kanji*, bright yellow Dutch clogs. They sent maps of where they'd been and circled where they were going. And the world was crowded with things that meant love.

Once she received a plain cedar box with a wooden knife inside, and she was disappointed for a long time. She felt the sentiment fell too far from love and into something much darker. She was not sure they could be sustained by such cruel gestures.

But then at the Paris flea market she found a beautifully carved antique music box. She brought it home and sculpted a little ballerina, lovely and lithe and wearing, of course, her smiling face. She snipped the plastic ballerina out of the box and put her own inside. She wouldn't dance, but he would recognize a clumsy sort of hope here, the echo of his very first gift to her.

And so the gifts continued, from Brussels to Tokyo, from Lodz to Buenos Aires, from Ankara to Johannesburg. Wood and clay went by boat, by air, by train. Each gift arrived with a slip, printed with only a new address. Messages slower but more powerful than those carried in the digital noise of the world. They never spoke, never wrote, never texted, never exchanged a photograph, though they sculpted and carved each other many times. They could not help but notice each grew lovelier in memory, even as they grew older and older in life.

Eventually, he went to sleep one night in a hotel bed in Heidelburg, and he never awoke again. The room was full of beautiful objects, the hotel maid saw; souvenirs, she supposed. She found a curious item next to his body: a plaster arm—a woman's arm with fingers curled as if around some object. No one on the hotel staff could tell if the hand was giving or receiving—or if it was beckoning something or someone to finally come home.

Birds with Teeth

He is thinking about Cope's skull. His rival issued the challenge publicly: Let us compare sizes! Let us see whose brain is bigger at last! But Marsh doesn't like the idea of his skull floating about the university labs, unmoored from its lonely body. Let Cope live on, headless with his challenge; Marsh will go to his grave a whole corpse.

He mourns alone in the breakfast room, slicing hard-boiled eggs and sprinkling them with pepper, watches dots darken the white like locusts over clouds. He imagines Cope's skull, grin stretched across like a rictus.

Your rope trick: you used to take out your own false teeth, grinning like a skull to entertain the Indians. You were a beautiful fool. Everyone loved you, even my own research assistants, everyone but me. There is no room for love in a boxing match, no room for affection in a street brawl. No room when the score was always so close.

—

But years ago, before the war began, there was room. They talked for hours at Haddonfield, grinning in helpless academic passion and exclaiming at their own twin hearts. They ate breakfast together on a heap of rock in the marl pits, black bread and coffee as the sun swam into the sky. Cope in shirtsleeves, a boy's face, looking more like Marsh's son than his contemporary.

I was a child once, and yet in so many ways I was never a child. I was a farmhand, and my father's only use for me was as a simple body, up before dawn to milk the cows, feed the pigs and chickens, muck out the stalls and troughs. I don't remember playing. I think now that I never played. I think that I was never a child.

◆

Cope, the child prodigy, cutting up lizards and snakes; Cope, the child-man, the Quaker with his "thee"s and "thou"s and the broad smile Marsh hated, even as he longed to crawl under its canopy. Cope smiled too much. He was too open, like a pilgrim sleeping on the road.

◆

Raw boy, with your Hadrosaurus foulkii, *coming out of your first triumph; you were soft as a baby. The pits were still rich with fossils then. You cannot blame me for seeing that you needed hardening. You and your smiles needed steeping in sap, needed polymerizing. You needed toughening, green shoot. This was a cutthroat business. This was a bone rush.*

◆

There were roses the day the woman left Marsh. Toppled over in the fight, petals scattered across the tiled floor. It looked like a love scene, not a fresco over the fringes of violence. She gasped and gasped like her life was falling away, like it was pouring out of her, a waterfall of hurt and astonishment. Stop breathing, he said, again and again. Stop breathing. Stop breathing.

⬦

You came to the Continent, Cope, full of rage and sadness that you twisted into a hunger for learning. We loved each other instantly, I think we did; I showed you Berlin and you spoke of that first trip to Boston when you were seven, spoke of the whales and how you'd drawn hopeful pictures of the harpooners at work. You'd wanted to see what a whale hunt looked like.

I told you about the cows and pigs and the way my uncle saved my life, appeared suddenly like Athena to Perseus, offered a world outside that small island. You told me about her, *how your father didn't approve, how he sent you to Europe to keep you out of her clutches as much as the army's. We drank together and ate together and debated together, and we stepped on one another's words in an eagerness to spill them all out. And when we returned to the States, we remembered. You named an amphibian fossil* Ptyonius marshii, *after me, and I named a new serpent* Mosasaurus copeanus, *after you. I think we did love one another. I truly think we did.*

⬦

Both discovered pterodactyls on their first trips out West. Marsh took measurements, sketched it, pushed it into the pages of the scientific journals. Dry bones on a dead thing. Cope, though, gave the monster life. He was one of the first to do so, to bring these New World fossils a stunning, bright sense of existence. "These strange creatures," he wrote, "flapped their leathery wings over the waves, and often plunging, seized many an unsuspecting fish; or, soaring, at a safe distance, viewed the sports and combats of more powerful saurians of the sea. At night-fall, we may imagine them trooping to the shore, and suspending themselves to the cliffs by the claw-bearing fingers of their wing-limbs."

In my reports, I detailed my discoveries, drew pictures of the new species, the shape and size of the bones. You wrote of the desolate wilderness, how ancient seashells littered the ground, how the jawbones of monsters hung hungry from the limestone cliffs. You always were a better writer. You always had a bit of the showman in you.

This is love for me, she said. I am not a good woman, she said. I am the end of all things, she said. This was at the beginning.

He shook his head. You are life, he said, and I invite you in.

She twisted her bracelet and smiled, thin gold band over those sweet white wrists traced with blue. Like Lilith? she asked. She had the thinnest skin, like paper; it was, she said, passed down from her mother, an Irish whore who birthed her in a brothel. I marveled at all that had been handed down from mother to daughter, all that was seeded and grown in the offspring: the thin white skin and the high blue veins and the gold hair and the talent for being the wrong kind of woman. No wonder Cope's father had chased her away. She was the kind of sickness a man would give anything to feel.

I wanted to see the graves of monsters, she said, mouth pointed downward, when I said I could not take her on the next expedition. I said no, many times, until she put her perfumed hand over my mouth. Because I am not quite a lady? she asked.

Because I am not quite a gentleman, I murmured from under her sweet palm, and she flung her arms around me and I could feel her smile press my cheek.

❧

Aug 31 1880

My dear Prof. Marsh,

I received some time ago your very kind note of July 28th, and yesterday the magnificent volume. I have looked with renewed admiration at the plates, and will soon read the text. Your work on these old birds on the many fossil animals of N. America has afforded the best support to the theory of evolution, which has appeared within the last twenty years. The general appearance of the copy which you have sent me is worthy of its contents, and I can say nothing stronger than this.

With cordial thanks, believe me yours very sincerely,
Charles Darwin

❧

We were still young when we set about proving we were done with gods.

❧

The West is full of a new kind of wild freedom. How can that compare with paved streets, a good restaurant, a vast library, a beautiful woman waiting in one's bed come moonlight? The West is full of painted skies, of sharp blues hanging over a sepia landscape. The West is full of vibrant cruelty, of dangerous and beautiful things.

❧

Our bodies were flamed like the oil lamps, bones underneath rattling with the force of the explosion. At the climax, she puffed her cheeks out and smiled with her mouth and eyes squeezed shut, like she was holding her breath. An old trick, she said; she learned it from a "friend" long ago. It makes it better, she said. More powerful. She was still shuddering as if to demonstrate the truth of this.

A pink foot poking out from beneath a sheet. A bosom rising and falling. Golden hair fanned over a white linen pillow.

You see, there are bad women who like good men, she told me.

I'm not good, I said. I just prefer a quiet heart.

I would prefer a new heart altogether, she said, and her eyes were like old stars as she spoke; echoes of stars burned out eons ago.

❖

It really began at Haddonfield, after he pointed out Cope's dreadful mistake with the *Elasmosaurus platyurus*. The head is on the tail, he told the team in private. He knows how it looked, knows how Cope and his temper took it. But he didn't intend to embarrass him, truly, though it was the beginning of the end. It was something too much for Cope, a needle in the throat. Cope's fierce rage would always be meant for Marsh, now.

❖

All the nights spent with her wrapped round his chairs, round his sheets, round his tall, portly body. All those nights covered in dewy flesh, in violets and jasmine and glasses of wine. Nights of open windows, of soft air in waves, of dreams punctuated by crickets and faint piano wafting up from the dance hall.

He knows what they say at the club, at the university, at the dig sites in the Badlands. They say he cannot feel affection. They say Marsh, why, he is impossibly cold. They would be astounded to learn what music his nights are made of, how he has learned to love a fallen woman like a fallen angel. How he has learned that they are nearly one and the same.

❧

Cope spent far more time than Marsh did away at the digs, glaring at the bleached white, the bones an open puzzle. With him always: an obsessive, complete journal of Marsh's perceived misdeeds. Every one of them recorded faithfully in that terrible, cramped handwriting. Cope never had the handwriting of a naturalist, despite all his training.

Marsh thinks they are related to birds, he wrote.

Marsh has stolen another discovery.

Marsh has bribed my men to turn over the larger fossils to him.

Marsh does not properly document his finds. He does not keep his books separate as he should.

Marsh has stolen her, *now. I hear she has stopped seeing other clients. Another set of bones once mine, now his.*

The sap and smoke and soot waft down the river in Hartford, and Marsh pours another glass of brandy. It is his fourth tonight. He has tired of reading about Cope's latest expedition. He will ask her to come to him. She will open him up and suck out the hurt, like a snakebite.

❧

We were on a large liner at sea, the black sky falling on us like a blanket. I dreamt of hipbones and sockets, of locks and keys. She drew her dream for me: she was lying in bed, when a great wall of water swept over her and dissolved bedding, nightgown, underthings, left her naked in the salty damp of the water's wake. She tried to move but the wall of water returned, it hurt, it scalded, and she was trapped like a fly in amber as it hardened, as it cooled and cracked. And there you were, Othniel, she said, there you were, chipping away with your hammer and chisel, trying to free me, and when you did my body was ruined, blackened, nothing but burnt bits. And you put me back together, pins through my bones, and stuck me in a case at your museum.

❖

Then there was the time the two teams came upon one another in the Como Bluffs and threw shouts, then insults, then stones, until their ears and fingers bled. Until they were covered in bruises and little red stars.

❖

We gave the same damn species thirty-some names. You published seventy-six academic papers in one year. I acquired so many fossils I'll never have time to look at them all, to open the crates and unpack the bones. They called it wasteful, useless. We called it love. We called it the rush to greet our long-lost dead.

❖

She finally left Marsh, the only way she knew. She was losing her insides by then, scarlet flowers in all her white handkerchiefs, so she went out West, where he had always promised her they'd go. Only she went alone, and she never came back. He learned of her death from a telegram, sent from a sanitarium in Arizona.

He heard that Cope's wife and daughter had left him, also. One of the side effects, evidently, of their mutual hunger for bones. He tried one more trick: to take Cope's fossils, to commandeer them for the government. It was the end of the end for Cope. For both of them, really. Cope turned over his catalogue of Marsh's misdeeds. The headline: SCIENTISTS WAGE BITTER WARFARE. Congress investigated and eventually saw an opportunity to eliminate the department of paleontology at the Geological Survey, along with Marsh's position as its head. Woe and wickedness, said one of Marsh's assistants, and he cried as they packed up the lab. Then he went to work for Cope, until Cope ran out of money, too.

❖

That ass in Congress shouting about birds with teeth, birds with teeth, are we taxpayers funding such a foolish blasphemy? And the other jackals taking up the cry. It has me in a black and dangerous mood, the brandy not enough to keep the devil from my tongue tonight.

❖

He eats the last of his egg, finishes his coffee, and reads the rest of the obituary. Small pleasures now, small hurts, too. He dabs at his beard with a napkin, feels his breath come shorter these days.

My own grave will be ready for me soon.

❖

I have heard about your nightmares, he almost wrote to Cope, years ago, but he tore the paper out of the notebook and balled it up till the ink was smeared through. *Nightmares where the bones of the dead assemble themselves, where they dance and gambol and knock their joints together in his ears, eternal ringing sounds and terrifying laughter. Nightmares where the creatures we discovered hover over Cope's camp bed and keep watch like vultures.*

I have heard about your dreams, he tried then, and put his head down, suddenly old, suddenly tired down to his own weary bones.

——

Sometimes I long to go West again, to watch the prairie grass ripple and the wind blow history clean. Like we could take it all back, this whole sordid business of living, and just fall into dust. As I suppose, one day, we will.

For These Humans Who Cannot Fly

The annals of the German waiting mortuaries are a "damned" chapter of history; few people outside Germany know anything about these extraordinary establishments. Even German writers on the subject concentrate on architectural and social aspects and avoid the central questions: Why were these bizarre hospitals for the dead built? Why were they maintained for a period of more than a hundred years? Did they ever serve any purpose?

—FROM *BURIED ALIVE: THE TERRIFYING HISTORY OF OUR MOST PRIMAL FEAR*, BY JAN BONDESON

Every death is a love story. It's the goodbye part, but the love is still there, wide as the world.

When my wife died, I began to understand this. I began to build the death houses. The name is misleading, since these houses hold not only death but futures, possibilities, hopes that the end isn't the end. These are perhaps tall tales, but they stack up better than dead bodies and they burn longer than kindling. I sell these tales for the living, and for the dying, and I have done this since my wife flew away.

The story about my wife is a short and sad one, not so new or so tall. My wife was lovely, with a smile like the moon dipped in stars. When we first married, she would fit herself into the crook of my arm as we slept; she would write me love letters three times a day and slip them into pockets, under cushions, behind the backs of mirrors and along the linings of drawers. She loved animals even more than she loved me, and we always had a cat or two in the house along with the dogs, mice, chickens, hedgehogs, goats, and sometimes even pigs. We never had birds because my wife couldn't stand to see them caged.

She sang on the stage, but soon grew to fancy herself an actual songbird. She would chirp and whistle instead of speaking and flap her arms as though they were wings. She started digging worms out of the soft earth in the early mornings, crushing them with her moon-smile and leaving pink fleshy bits in her teeth. She would hop to the window on light feet and watch the birds in the trees, weeping because she couldn't join them in flight. She banished the cats from the house after one brought in a robin with its neck broken and dropped it on her pillow.

I have reached a milestone today. I have built exactly one hundred death houses, all over Europe and the United States. In those houses I've placed exactly five hundred Temporary Resting Containers, built to house the newly dead until they reawaken. Five in each house to start with. (The clients are free to build more, but I provide only five.) Five hundred love stories, begun at their ends. I do think of myself as a romantic. I think of myself as a false idol, or sometimes, a saint. Women often embrace me, and many offer me expensive gifts and sometimes more than that. Men shake my hand and choke up, clearing their throats. When I leave a village or a city with its very own death house, I can see it collectively sigh and relax, as if a great weight had been lifted from its massive shoulders. I can see the people's relief rising like smoke, the residue of tamped-down fear.

I usually choose a restful spot for the death house, or *Leichenhaus*. It should rise gracefully in an arc, casting a long shadow on cobblestones and hearts. But I try to keep things playful, too. In many villages, I find that placing it at the end of a long road and a short curve mimic the element of surprise when death arrives.

One morning my wife told me that on the river, bodies crash like a car wreck. She said she had been waiting at the high bridge, watching and studying the jumpers for years. She had discovered the sound was almost glacial, glassy, like somebody breaking hundreds of china plates all at once.

Your skull splits right open sometimes, she said.

I feel sorry for these humans who cannot fly, she said.

I will show them how it's done, she said.

So I put my lovely wife in a place where the windows were barred and the doors were locked, and where the bird-ladies that roamed the halls could find no worms to tear into.

I always assemble the finest materials and the most skilled workmen when building a death house, taking special care when choosing the images for the stained glass. I particularly prefer Gertrude, robed in a light, flat gray, or Margaret of Antioch, lines of blue cut glass flowing through her gown like small waves. St. Michael, too, makes an excellent guardian of the dead; I often put him in royal red with the Kingdom of Heaven as a backdrop. And always appropriate: St. Joseph, patron saint of a happy death.

❧

She wrote me letters just as before—three times a day, I discovered later. She never spoke but she could scratch out a few thoughts. The doctors who cared for her thought it best to keep these letters from me, as they contained useless scraps and musings, hopping from subject to subject and leaving sense entirely behind. The doctors seemed also to harbor vague suspicions about me; they seemed to believe something terrible had happened to tear out my wife's tongue like Philomela's.

I visited only once. My wife spent the visit tilting her head and chirruping at me in frustration. She finally ran at the only small window in the room, so many times that her head was bloodied and her hands and arms bruised all over. I tried to stop her but could not; she had become so small and light she could slip out of my arms as easily as she used to slip into them. I cried for the attendants and when I saw how they bound her, how they forced white pills into her small red mouth, I fainted and woke to find myself being driven home. I never returned.

❧

I usually construct the death houses as large, simple structures with gently sloping roofs. Sometimes there are cupolas. But I never use spires or flourishes or gargoyles. No stone creatures of any kind, in fact.

It's a matter of taste, of course, but I feel the death house should be much like a room in God's own house, and would God's house be a Gothic affair? Some of my clients seem to think so, but I can usually tempt them toward a more modest design. I make sure the building will stay dark and cool most of the time, and always include at least one large room for the dead and one small room for the watchman and his medical supplies.

◆

One day the hospital wrote to tell me my wife was dead. She had escaped from her room somehow and had discovered an open window in an office from which to fly. She had broken almost every bone in her body, they said. I imagined her, hovering at the window the way she had done at home, reaching up to separate the edges of her life like chaff from the ball of clouds—then plummeting. Would she have known? I wondered. Would she have realized halfway down, checking her thin shoulder blades, surprised like anything that the wings she thought she saw that morning seemed to have disappeared like smoke?

◆

I usually assist my employers in furnishing their *Leichenhaus*. The watchman's room is kept comfortable, but spare, to prevent sleeping on the job. I suggest a chair, a table, a light, and a pack of playing cards. Also a cot and a small first-aid kit for attending to the dead if they suddenly become the living. I always make sure the openness of the large hall is not marred by any unnecessary furnishings. Only the Temporary Resting Containers should lie in this hall. I usually recommend that customers limit the number of Containers, to keep unpleasant odors to a minimum.

Sometimes, when I arrive, the mayors of the towns drape medals around my neck. Sometimes they present me with the oversized keys to their cities. Someone important makes a speech, the citizens clap, and the local inn agrees to put me up for free. Once a local artist painted my picture and it hangs in the central courthouse, I am told, even to this day. I have grown elderly and weak but the local people still describe me in hero words wherever I go, whenever I come to save them from their deaths.

◆

I built the first *Leichenhaus* for my wife, of course. She was so damaged that they would not let me see her, not at first, but when I begged the doctors relented and brought me to the morgue. She was purple and black in places, and her head was a strange shape, and she looked flattened and out of joint, like a rag doll. But her pale face was still perfect, and her lips were still slightly O-shaped and pink, and her eyes were wide and sea-calm. She looked as though she were about to speak. So how could I bury her? I knew she was dead, of course I knew, but at the same time I doubted. She who had longed for sky and spurned four walls—how could I put her in a box? How could I shut her up in the earth with a face like that? I'd read Bruhier's best-selling pamphlet, *Dissertation sur l'incertitude des signes de la mort*. It detailed the various ways to determine if a loved one is really dead: stabbing the nose or feet with sharp objects, pouring vinegar into the mouth, holding the fingers over flame, placing a mirror over the mouth to detect breath, pulling the tongue to facilitate artificial respiration, etc. I went out of my head, I demanded the doctors perform every one of these procedures, I shouted that they would never bury or burn her.

Instead I built the first Temporary Resting Container, just for her. I used an ordinary coffin, and attached a three-foot cord to a

78

bell and a bell stand. I sawed off the top half of the coffin lid, and laid the remaining length of cord in the top half of the coffin itself. I laid her mangled body on the red velvet and tied the piece of cord to one swollen, broken finger. In case she woke, in case she rose, she could but move her finger and the bell would ring. To guard her I hired two former soldiers; around them I built a small shelter to keep out the rain and heat. I employed doctors to stay on call for seven days, ready at a moment's notice to rush to my wife's aid should she awaken. They all thought I was insane; I was insane. But after seven days, the madness left me in a rush and I consented to the burial of my wife. I was comforted. I was sure that the ending of our story was what it ought to be. I was sure it was really an ending.

❧

I always suggest placing the Temporary Resting Containers in the middle of a large hall, in a harmonious and pleasing arrangement. This allows corpses awakened during the day to take in the full majesty of the stained glass windows, and may help to counter feelings of terror and confusion. Although I do not provide them, I also suggest placing flower arrangements around the Resting Containers; this aids in covering the unpleasant odors of rot and decay with more pleasing scents like violet, rose, and peony.

I usually do the hiring myself as far as death house personnel are concerned. I hire two to four watchmen, depending on the size of the facility, to guard the hall and administer medical aid if necessary. I look for watchmen who are alert, healthy, strong, incurious, and possessed of little or no imagination. This is very important, as it would be very bad for business if one of the watchmen frightened himself to death in a death house. The watchmen must also be trained a little in medicine, in case any simple emergency medical procedure need be performed before a doctor could be summoned. Basic first-aid training usually suffices.

❖

I was a young man when my wife died. I am an old man now, and I am ready for death myself. I have built one hundred death houses and I have seen countless love stories ended and begun. I have become an expert in managing death, in easing life into sleep into death into darkness. It's a slow process, but a good process. A necessary one.

And no, no one really comes back from the dead. Even in my beautiful, carefully built Leichenhausen. Even when the sun pours from the Kingdom of Heaven through St. Michael's stained glass robes and shines on the faces of the dead like rubies, like wine, like blood.

Take Your Daughter to the Slaughter

Our fathers wake us before dawn. They wake us and we rise, confused at first, and then excited, remembering what today is. Remembering what we will become, with a little practice, a little patience. A steady eye and hand.

Today is the opening day of werewolf season. Today we leave our dresses, our heels, our crinolines and crystals in the closet, and we take our camouflage out of storage. We check the contents of our daypacks: map, matches, knife, first-aid kit, water, trail mix, tree-stand safety belt, compass. We shower and spray ourselves down with odor neutralizer.

We don our Blaze Orange vest and check our ammo, fingering the bright rows of silver bullets, pretty and promising as the moon. If we bring down a werewolf, we get to dig the bullets out and string them on a necklace like bloody, lumpy beads. Some of the older girls have necklaces so long they drape them round two, three times, like strands of pearls.

When we set up our stands, we feel a little fear, an icicle thrill at the thought of teeth and claws. We know that if we slip up, we could be bitten, we could be killed. We know that we could fail. It is important; it is vital to our town that we succeed. We have spent the year learning how to use our rifles, diligently attending target practice after school, at shooting ranges and on decoys in the fields, when the weather allows.

Some of us feel sorry for the werewolves. Some of us do not want to kill, the soft thunk of bullet in flesh a thing apart from the hard clean splintering of wood and paint. Our fathers remind us of what we already know: the werewolves are a pestilence, a plague upon our forests, and killing them makes a good sport and a kind deed. There are too many werewolves, our fathers tell us; if we do not cull the herd they will starve to death come winter. They will spread disease and decay.

This is what fathers and daughters have always done in our towns, they say. This is a good and righteous way to live. And so we nod, and learn the proper way to clean our rifles, to use a compass, to scout a location, to field-dress a dead werewolf. And so we come, every year in our time, to the hunt.

We crouch beside our fathers in the brush. We hold our breath; we watch a family of werewolves rip the meat from a deer carcass in the clearing. We are silent and still. We are eager to prove that we are good daughters.

One large wolf, a male, leaves the pack and ambles toward us. We shiver in the cold and the tight grip of fear; a small girl was eaten only last year, her father helpless to act as she was dragged away by a furious and wounded wolf. We blink, blink, and here the wolf stops, sniffing, and here is an unobstructed broadside shot, and here are our fathers mouthing, Shoot, shoot! and here is our shot flying true and flaying skin and muscle just below the shoulder. Here is the unearthly howl, and our blood freezes to our bones to hear it. Here is the werewolf, here is the glassy-eyed stare, here is the twitch and the moan and here is the carcass on the ground and our fathers' hands on our shoulders, strong and proud. Here is our first kill.

With the help of our fathers, we dress the werewolf and drag it to our trucks. Later, we will dig the bullets out and string them, silver over our throats. Later, we will eat the hearts of the men they slowly become; we will share this meat with our fathers and we will warm our shame at that howl, our sadness at that last dissolve of paw to hand. Our fathers will hold their palms up and smile.

We Were Holy Once

We Benders got headaches in our blood, the way some people got brains or beauty. Me and Katie are both sore afflicted, not only with the headaches but also with dizziness and fainting spells, too. And sometimes we get to feeling sick in the stomach, and sometimes we even get bright, blurred colors, right at the edge of our seeing, like watching a rainbow through window glass.

Katie makes use of hers because she's the actress of the family. That's what Pa says. She calls herself Professor Miss Katie and whenever we move to a new town, we put out that she is a soothsayer. And when one of her fits comes upon her, she makes sure to faint right near a crowd of folks and come up talking about some spirit what was trying to contact a loved one nearby. Everybody knows somebody dead.

That's how we drum up business. That and also Pa and Ma put out some tables and chairs on one side of our cabin, and strung up a bedsheet so customers can have some privacy, and there's a cot if they want to sleep as well as dine. And Professor Miss Katie is also Doctor Miss Katie and if folks want a healer, she's good for that, too.

Katie Bender is full of the talents that never got born in other people, that's what Pa says. And Ma frowns and says nothing at all, but that's just Ma for you.

◆

How it works is this: One of the townsfolk don't trust doctors, and maybe they got a good reason not to, so they come and ask for Doctor Miss Katie instead. They know that title don't mean Doctor like schooling, but Doctor like healing, helping folks get well. Katie has a lot of different charms and spells she uses. Her favorite is something she calls the Quick Healer—it's supposed to speed up the getting-better part of being sick. She has a little cherry wood cabinet that Pa made before he got hurt, real pretty with carvings of fruits and nuts spilling from horns of plenty. She's got it filled with dried herbs, and she chooses different ingredients from different drawers depending on what ails you. She grinds them together with a mortar and pestle, and mixes that with soap and ashes to make a paste. Sometimes she sort of sings while she mixes, her yellow hair hanging down in sheets over her face, her arms twitching with the effort of all that grinding and stirring. She sing-hums charms against death, against poison and rot, against the damp and cold and the evil that lurks outside the door. I don't much like the song and I don't like watching her sing it, like a backwoods witch. It makes my skin itch and my head hurt, but I always watch her anyway. It hurts not to watch her, that's how bright she is, like light off glass. She mixes all kinds of things: waybread, cockspur, chamomile, nettle. Fennel and crab apples and lamb's cress and dandelion. Milk and honey and burdock, to make the crops grow and the livestock strong.

I think she makes most of it up. I used to think Katie really *was* some kind of healer, until one day I watched her humming and muttering and mixing, her hair down and her back to the anxious little fellow waiting for his ma's medicine. And just for a second the front of her face poked through the hair and she winked at me, bold as brass. How it works is this: Katie Bender is a good liar and a very good actress and how it works, also, is this: People will believe just about anything that comes out of a pretty girl's mouth.

I'm not much for acting, and not much good at lying, so Pa says it's best to pretend I am dumb and that is just what I do. When we get to a town, we put it out how Katie's a seer and we put it out that I'm not right in the head. It helps because people say all kinds of things around an idiot that they wouldn't say around anyone else. Idiots must have an awful lot of good secrets. I'm a good listener and I remember most things people say; I tuck them away in the drawers in my head and label them careful so later I can go back and pull out the things I need to know. Like who has just came into a large inheritance, or who has money socked away under the mattress, or who has lost a loved one and would pay good gold to speak to them again. So I come in useful, too, even though I can't act for beans and I can't do the German accent, neither.

The accent was Pa's idea. He said nobody in these little frontier towns would know Germany from Georgia so it was fine if it didn't come off perfect. It's easier to explain why we just came here so sudden, with a decent bit of money, and no people to speak of. Katie taught us all the way to speak, funny and short with sounds like you're choking on a bite of beef. Pa and Ma are pretty good, and Katie sounds positively foreign. She is forever making us proud, plus she's real pretty too, with lots of yellow hair and teeth what look like rich folks' teeth, white and straight and shiny. Half my teeth have fell out already, and Pa has only two teeth left in his whole head; he uses them to open cans and crack nuts. Which he does pretty often. He likes to show off them teeth, as Ma says, like a sideshow freak. Ma doesn't believe in being prideful. Katie's a lot more like Pa. Pa says whatever you do, you should be the best at it. And I think we are.

⬦

How it works is this: We set up something called a séance in the dining room. It sounds fancy, but it just means a meeting with dead people. We move all the tables out, and Pa and me drag in the big table and the medium's chair from the shed out back. Pa built that chair special for Katie, with a false back where she keeps the things she needs. I always sit next to Katie so we can both keep a hand free. I'm an important part of the séances. When all the people come in— no more than six because our little cabin just ain't that big—we get them sat down and douse all the lights. It's always at night because it has to be real dark, black as molasses hung right over the moon, so nobody can see a thing except for what we want them to. Katie's got a whole bag of tricks. She can do voices, so sometimes she'll speak in a high, soft child's voice. Sometimes she'll do a woman, but deep-voiced and brassy, a warm, twangy kind of voice. That voice always makes me a little sad, because she sounds like someone it would be awful nice to know—someone kind and with a sound of home about them.

Sometimes I'm supposed to open the false panel and pull out the fishing pole, and attach a letter or a handkerchief or some other white thing to it, and wave it about until the visitors all go into hysterics. Katie has a lever she works with her foot—it hooks into the bottom of the table and she can make the table tip this way and that, and the ladies all scream and gasp at that one. My favorite, though, is the bell trick. Katie puts a little gold bell smack in the middle of the table, a little glass dome over top of it. You can see it all through the séance, not moving, even while you hear the muffled sounds of a bell ringing out. It's a pretty spooky effect, and of course nobody thinks that maybe Katie's got a bell hidden away in that panel, wrapped in a piece of muslin so's to make that muffled sound. It's a real good trick.

After the séance, the women usually cry and the men shuffle their feet and look at the floor, and everybody calls Katie a miracle and gives her lots of money. She just smiles and smiles, my pretty sister, and all the while you can see her green eyes filling up with cash.

❧

At bedtime Katie used to tell me stories about how we were, us people, a long time ago. How we were all holy once. How the earth was full of plenty, how everybody loved everybody, and how there was no sin. And how nobody went hungry, and how people were kind and gentle, even to the animals. And how a woman went and ruined it all for everybody else.

Ain't that just like a woman, I would say, and roll my eyes like Pa when he talks about god. And Katie would laugh, and pretend to cuff me, and instead she'd muss my hair and tell me to be off to bed. Ain't it just, she'd say, and she would smile the kind of smile she uses for the strangers who come to our place and do not ever leave it.

❧

How it works is this: When a guest comes to stay the night, Ma and Katie string up the curtain splitting our little cabin in two. Pa and I bring the tables in, and Ma and Katie make them look real nice with clean white tablecloths and fresh cut wildflowers from the field out back. Ma makes a hearty dinner, with fried potatoes and steak and soda biscuits, and a dried apricot pie for dessert. Katie brings out a glass of good whisky, wearing the kind of dress barmaids at the Blue Saloon would blush at. But Pa says it's for the greater good. He says everything is for the greater good, and that we shouldn't feel bad about these men, these fat, lonely men who worship nothing but money and god. I'm too afraid of Pa and his black pinprick eyes to ask him anything. But once I asked Ma what he worshipped and she scowled at me and said I was a fool. So I think maybe he doesn't worship anything, and I suppose that I don't either. Or maybe I just worship Pa. Maybe worship and afraid is the same thing.

Anyhow there's Katie in her tight blue bodice, making sure the men's eyes are on her all the time, and she's pouring whisky down their gullets. And there's me, opening the trapdoor right behind the chair and there's Pa, coming up swinging his sledgehammer, and there's Ma with the rope, binding their hands, and there's Katie with the big butcher knife, slicing the throat clean open just like you'd kill a hog. And I suppose in a way, they are like hogs, and ever since we all fell down from Eden we're animals, all of us, turning on each other every day. Only some folks like us Benders just do it more direct. Or maybe we're just better at it.

❦

If we fell so long ago, Katie says, it could hardly be our fault that we went bad. But long ago seems like not that long ago to me. Long ago, Katie and I went to school, and we studied hard, and I thought maybe I would be a carpenter like Pa, or that maybe I would go into the army and learn to fight and use a gun. And long ago the world was small enough, and big enough, and we had friends and Pa did a good trade and even Ma would smile now and then. I'm not too sure when long ago became just now, but it happened too quick for me to notice. I think sometimes maybe it was when Pa hurt his hand, or maybe it was when our little sister Susan died so sudden of the measles, or maybe it was when me and Katie started fainting, and the townsfolk started giving us the sideways eye. In any case, somewhere in between long ago and now, we learned how it works. We got smart.

❧

How it works is this: They come for us at dawn, sun up like an egg, the raw, angry posse with fists around guns and torches and knives. We cleared out in time, because we're smart, we're Benders, and we're always one step ahead. We leave behind the bodies in the orchard and we take the money—some ten thousand by Pa's reckoning—and we light out in the wagon just before daybreak. Later they brag, that posse, they tell all kinds of tales: they found us and they beat us all to death; they found us and they skinned us all alive; they found us and they shot us all or burned us all or fed us all to starving coyotes. They gave us to the savages who beat time with our bones.

But none of this is true. How it works is this: We're always going to be one step ahead. We see things most folks can't. We see the dead, and we see the real ugly souls of the living. And we see better in the dark than you.

La Belle de Nuit, La Belle de Jour

This is the troubled edge of the kingdom. It is rumored that dragons sleep near, just off the coast of our dreams. Our days are short, and our troubles grow along with the darkness. We are alone and mad here in our isolation. We live in heaps of blight and scarce, scraggly vegetation, good for nothing but lighting our fires. Our trees are all dead; the branches crack and snap like brittle bones.

It was not always like this. Once this was a green place, full of memory and music. Once it was, perhaps not paradise, but clean, whole, a lively place at least. There was a sense that things were growing, becoming. There were so many rhymes then, so many songs, burbling up from the soil and rivers like laughter. I was training to be a singer myself, learning to sound both the new and also the ancient notes, learning to weave the stories of the kingdom's heroes into complex melodies. My brothers were learning to be great kings, like the kings of the days long past. There was a sense that the people were renewing themselves, and the people dreamed of a golden age come again to the world. On our days off, my brothers and I hunted and fished and swam and flew our kites. We took pictures of one another, my eldest brother always pulling faces and making our parents laugh. On our favorite days, my youngest brother and I would drive to the great shore and feed the swans, watching them gracefully sail through water like small white ships.

But then one day the rumors reached us: a great and terrible witch was on her way. And the earth seemed to shrivel and wither. And the animals disappeared under the ground and over the hills. And one sad day, I stood in the doorway of our castle and watched the last of the birds winging away, the sky a pale and eerie red as they flew. Even our beloved swans left us.

Many of our people burned in the great fires, sacrifices to the gods that might stop the witch's coming. I always thought I would end up among them, there in the center of the cypress husks, but my father forbade me go and my mother was too ill to be alone with so many sons to care for. And so I watched my friends dance in the fires, falling one by one to ash as the skies grew gray and the smoke filled the heavens with haze. Of course it didn't work. She arrived just the same, stepping off the jet in her fur coat and sunglasses, a beautiful, haughty, horrible thing. We watched on TV, the cameras snapping away, her strange made-creatures ringing her like clay golems. When the cameras zoomed in, you could see the thumbprint on their foreheads, the dead, awful eyes, the huge hands. She waved to the curious crowds and smiled like Morgana, and got in her car and headed straight for our kingdom. We stopped dreaming that night for good. We started to fall under her spell, one by one, until only my brothers and I remained untouched.

And then, one horrible afternoon, just three days after we buried my mother, my father married Her. The queen of darkness, *la belle de nuit*, lady of the last days. She brought his soul through hell and fire and made it hers.

The first thing she asked for was the moon. Then the sky-stained stars. Then the canvas of the sky itself. My brothers rose up in anger at that, left in a pack to hunt and bring back a boar's head that looked like hers. They left me alone and I was angry, terrified. The eldest said they would be back soon, and smiled, and said not to worry. The youngest looked back at me, and frowned, and warned me to stay out of her sight while they were away. But that same afternoon she put deadly toads in my bath and snakes in my skirt. Only the warnings of the servants saved me. She poisoned my words so they left my lips as bees, stinging my throat and tongue so badly I thought I would die. And she reached out with her mild blue eyes and turned my brothers to seven wild swans, in mockery of the creatures that meant the most to us.

I went to my father, tried to plead with him, but the bees left my lips and my father, horrified, pronounced me a demon. She smiled, and nodded, and summoned her minions, those terrible dark hulking things. They circled me and grabbed me and their hands hurt like ice. They did terrible things to me, and when they had finished, they wiped the blood on their pinstriped trousers and drove my body to the shore. And there they released me, gave me to the waves to claim and keep.

But I was not dead, not quite. My breath rippled the water, my remaining fears flew straight up like a flare, a bright column of stars. I was mute and all alone, underneath the cold moon, on the deserted white road it shone over the sea. The thunder—hers or nature's, I could not tell—was deafening and I flung myself forward, seeing no land in sight, hearing no sound that could save me. At last, just before the end of my strength had come, I smashed against a tall rock, and I half-clambered, half-floated onto it and collapsed over its welcome solid stern.

Suddenly a single white feather landed beside me. As I gazed up, I saw seven swans winging down, furiously beating against the winds, coming to land neatly in a circle around me. I was surrounded again, but this time by my brothers, my poor, poor brothers, just boys, and how I wept to see them changed so, and how they wept to see me broken so, and how we stayed on that rock for many days, exhausted and alone and utterly devoid of hope or home. They brought me fish and fresh water to build back my strength, and the tears they wept healed my wounds and wore away my scars. And on the seventh day, I woke, healthy and whole, to find my brothers human and solemn and sleeping beside me.

I woke them, unable to speak for the spell on me, but shaking them and humming and grunting with a sort of primitive delight. My eldest brother shouted and smiled, but the youngest frowned and told me this would only last a day. On the last day of each month, he said, the witch had told him they would spend the day as humans once more—not out of kindness, but out of cruelty, so that they would always know the terrible thing that had happened and would remember the human bodies they could never possess again. We wept again this time, and yet again when I shook my head and tried to speak and the bees escaped their prison. We knew I must be parted from my brothers during the day, for they must hunt upon the water and I must live upon the land. And so they brought a cast-off fishing net, and carried me in it to the edge of the water, where I was able to stand and walk and search for a place to live. I found a sort of a cave at the edge, in a little grotto, and in it I made a home, as best I could, and spent the days sleeping and dreaming of music and sunshine and my brothers and I as we were. And at night I lay near the water, to watch over my brother-swans as they nestled their heads in their necks and floated their way to a sad, undreaming sleep.

All the while, the witch was building her city. Her fortress of stone stood at the base of our village, with ten enormous guns to guard it and ten thousand goons to defend it. Our castle became a prison, and the villagers who hadn't fled one by one started to disappear inside it. The first to go were the fanatics, then the political dissidents, but eventually a problem arose: she needed an army to go east and take back outposts that had been ours in my great-great-grandfather's time. So the peasants started disappearing, too, but some were able to get messages out and usually they said simply "GONE EAST TO FIGHT."

And so the villagers began to hide. They built rabbit-like warrens and underground dens; they went south and dug caves there, or went further south to the next kingdom. The artists fled, the musicians fled, the actors fled, the politicians fled, the merchants and craftsmen fled, and our city was finally empty and silent. But she was not content with this. She would have subjects to worship her, an army to command. And so at last she began to build her ghosts. An army of chemically broken once-bodies, she build them of the newly dead, the long-dead, and even the inhuman-dead—snouts and hooves and long hairy tails hooked to human arms and legs and faces. It became not uncommon to see a soldier with the head of a sheep, or a goat, or a bull. The animal eyes rolled in terror and the nostrils snorted in short bursts and the bellows of beastly fear groaned from furry, foam-covered muzzles. But the bespelled human body marched on, and on, and on, off to certain sacrifice in the east. The kings that ruled there were horrified by the black magic advancing on their kingdoms, and they ordered that any animal-man captured alive was to be staked through the heart and decapitated immediately. Then the body and head would be burned in a pit, setting the poor souls at rest once more.

But despite the brutality of these measures, the witch was still winning. She could conjure endless soldiers from the dead, enough to circle the world and back again. By day she sat in her throne room and traced their routes on maps and laughed, bare throat thrown back, barbed wire stretched around her throne for protection. By night she threw lavish, wicked parties for all the humans she had in her power, the ones who had remained fixed by her charms. Her court feasted every night for hours, on course after course, while the rest of the kingdom starved: ground meat in spiced wine sauce; meatballs in aspic; pork pottage; bladders full of eggs, pepper, cloves, currants, dates, and sugar in a rich sauce; roast venison, baby rabbit, stork, crane, buzzard, peacock, partridge, woodcock, egret; a course of martinets baked in quinces; wine, apples, and pears with sugar and syrup fruit compote; cherries and grapes; and finally a cheese course with spiced red wine and wafers. Where she got all of this abundance, no one knew, but by the lean look of her court much of it must have been enchanted.

After these feasts, she held elaborate masked balls with champagne fountains, and hired jazz bands to play wild, whirling tunes. Speakers were placed in the courtyard to carry the sound of the revelry far and wide. Handsome men and beautiful women danced until dawn in tails and beads and sequins. In the shadows of the halls and courtyard, bodies tangled in hot, animal passions, sometimes three and four and ten or twenty. Sometimes these orgies went on for days, it was rumored. But, some said, if you removed the participants' masks, you would see red eyes, haggard faces, sweat-soaked brows and deathly pallor. Help us, they would mouth, cracked, bleeding lips working around the hopeless words.

One of these nights, as I slept on the cold ground near the water, I could hear the music and see their poor faces, these trapped souls. I dreamt of their pleas, and her laughter, and I heard her then, clear as day, whisper the secret of my release into my father's unhearing ear. She told him he must order all the flax in the kingdom brought and burned, for if I was ever able to weave seven shirts of the stuff—one for each of my brothers—they would return to human form and all her magic would be undone. In the dream, my puppet-father nodded, and I cringed as she kissed his lifeless lips, licking at the bits of soul that still cling there, like strands of honey. She smiled, all red mouth and sharp teeth and white, white face like the coldest moon. And I woke and knew exactly what I must do.

We cannot wait for mercy to fall from heaven, I told my brothers. They flew up to avoid the bees and gave me swanlike, skeptical stares when I described my dream, each syllable stinging my lips like needle pricks. But should we do nothing, I cried, and I think then they knew it was harder for me than it was for them; harder for the human to spend a lifetime waiting than for the immediate needs of the animal creatures to be met. And so when the sun left the sky and the trees drank from the earth, when brimstone pools ringed the cave where I lay, my brothers would gather the flax I needed from the farthest reaches, leaving it for me to find in neat piles when I woke. And so I began to weave, and so we began to hope.

In the beginning, the cave seemed a haunted place, almost an old abandoned drawing room, grown oppressive with damp and rot. I heard laughing. Bats swept unseen overhead like ghosts; cobwebs grew thick over the walls like damask drapery. The air was dark and heavy, full of a strange animal musk I couldn't place—rather like a long-dead lady's perfume.

But eventually we grew to understand one another, my cave and I. I grew comfortable, unafraid, trusted to fate and my task. And I went on doing all I could to plait the flax and weave the shirts, my hands a mess of cuts and oozing sores, my hair a tangled, filthy mat. I used the laces of my boots to knot it back, and then eventually I lost my boots, too, and went barefoot in the wild. My feet grew callused and hard, my lips grew swollen and red from the occasional uttered sound and ensuing stings. I must have looked more animal than human to any passersby, though I never saw any other humans in this secluded place. Not until the day the foreign king drove through.

His car was a shiny gray, sleek and modern and so out of place in this wild, ancient wood. It looked like an industrial beast fleeing unthinkable places, the new cowering from the oldest things of the world. And the man who drove it belonged in a very modern magazine; he was all black hair and sharp lines and tan, so tan and healthy it hurt my sick eyes to look for too long. It was like looking at the sun. I wondered, briefly, madly, if I was gazing at some incarnation of Apollo and his chariot, lighting my woods for a moment on their way to somewhere else. But then he stopped his car. He and his companion, a short man with kind eyes, who reminded me of my smallest brother. They got out of the car and ran to where I was frozen in the act of picking the nettles for the shirts. Apollo-who-was-not-Apollo tilted his head to the side and did the thing men do when they decide they are falling in love. And I dropped my flax nettles, horrified, and ran back to the cave in hopes of losing these invaders.

They followed me, of course, and used their artificial light to find their way down the dark. And you know, everyone knows, how the story unfolds when a man decides he is in love. A very stupid man, clearly; who decides to love a wild and probable imbecile, a feral child scraping the ground for plant scraps? But men in the throes of their own passion do odd things. And this, of course, was our neighboring king, more used to following his passions than most. So you can guess, then, that he was the poor sort of king that leaves the running of his kingdom to others and spends his days hunting deer and fox and women with equal aplomb. So you can guess, then, how he took me, against the frowns and sager advice of his friend. You can guess how delighted he was by my refusal to speak, by the acquiescence signaled by the absence of a "no." You can guess, I'm sure, that after the bath, and the bandages, and the damask silk and pearls, and the fawning court ladies, and the leering court men—*You wear those robes like a courtesan*—and through it all, my weeping, weeping, weeping over my lost flax shirts, and my chance of saving my poor brothers gone for now if not for good—you can guess how he took me, how he stripped me of those new robes like an unwrapped present and how he hurt me terribly, fiercely, and how in his supreme arrogance he took my tears for gratitude and licked them with his neat pink tongue like a panther. Don't cry, he said, kindly, I suppose. This happiness will last, he said. And just like that, never mind the society ladies, the royal heirs lined up for the chance at his hand, never mind his father's wish that he marry a foreign princess—he disappointed court and country alike and married the wild young thing he'd found in the wood.

It was a danger from the start and he never saw it. It made people angry, and angry people are apt to start rumors that other angry people want to believe. It soon got around, even to my sheltered ears, that I was a wood spirit, an evil one, and that I spent half my time in fox shape and half in human shape. It was whispered that I had bewitched His Majesty. It was whispered that I turned him into a boar when he slept. It was whispered that I stole a piece of his soul every time he made love to me. And why not? I supposed it was no odder than the truth; and I was, yes, bewitched. I knew I could never, never let myself try to speak in front of these people, or they would burn me for witchcraft for sure.

I kept trying to get out to the cave, but I was virtually under lock and key. It was a large, modern kingdom, much less rustic than ours, and court life was quite structured. You were never, ever alone. Ladies and servants and hangers-on, and yet you were always lonely. The only person I wasn't lonely with was the King's friend, who reminded me so much of my youngest brother. He was very tender with me, and always made time to stop and talk to me in my walks through the gardens, or to take me out for drives because he knew how much I missed my wood. Though he thought I'd been there always, of course. I was glad of these trips, and I even liked the car—I had never ridden in one before and was surprised at how exhilarating the feeling of speed could be. The King never minded these outings—he spent most of his time hunting, and, I suppose, whoring and drinking. One late night when very drunk he forced open my mouth and pulled out my tongue. He told me there was nothing so wrong with me and demanded to know why I couldn't speak. I shook my head, again and again, and he said he would put my mouth to better use instead then. He wrapped my hair around his fist, around, and around, like a skein, and forced me to my knees, and I thought then of my poor brothers, doomed to fly over the waves for their long or short lives. Would they live as long as men, or as long as swans? How long do swans live? How long would I, with this brutish husband and a court composed of jealousy and lies?

Not long, not long as it happened, and it happened so quickly I am still dizzy now as I am tied to the stake. The thing I feared: in my sleep I spoke, or tried to, and my husband woke to swarms of bees flooding from my mouth and stinging his naked flesh. I was quickly denounced and dragged off, my hair shorn, a rough cotton gown thrown over me—and just when I'd given up all hope, sent up a silent message on the winds to my poor brothers—there in the prison with me, unbelievably, were my flaxen shirts and a large pile of nettles beside them! The jailor laughed and said that poor kind friend of the King's, he had brought them, for he knew how important they had been to me. He thought perhaps they would comfort me in my final hours. Though, added the jailor, you haven't got many more hours, witch—they'll be burning you at dawn. I made myself weave faster than I ever had before. I would save my brothers if I could not save myself. And I have been weeping and weaving; through the bumpy, sickening cart ride to the burning place; through the surprising heavy pain of the apples and pears and other rotten fruit heaved at me; through the cries of "witch," "harlot," "burn her," as the cart passed the throngs of villagers gathered to watch the fire—through all this I wove and I wept and I prayed to any god who would hear me to let me finish my work. And as they tie me to the stake I am on the very last shirt, and as they light the faggots below me, seven large, lovely white swans suddenly sail over the crowd and land in a circle surrounding me. I wince as the smoke hits my eyes and blindly I throw the flaxen shirts through the air, even the unfinished one. And because magic always works that way, they land, yes, they float, yes, softly over the heads of the swans and their feathers, and the shirts transform them at once into my dear handsome brothers again. All except for my youngest brother, whose shirt was unfinished and so still has a swan's wing instead of a man's arm, though other than that he is whole and human and hale. And then the flames flicker and fail, and the crowd gasps and slowly, slowly they began to bow, in waves they bow before these men they know now to be princes or angels or gods.

My brothers explain to the silent villagers who they are, and who I am, and I open my mouth to weep my brothers' names, and no bees emerge, no, nothing but the sweet sound of the human, very human sound of my youngest brother's name, after the archangel himself, and indeed he as gentle and forbearing in his deformity now as if he were still in flight over the endless sea.

The Men and Women Like Him

It's raining when Hugh arrives at the gates of Jerusalem, and the skirmish is already well under way. Roman legionnaires are hacking at faceless creatures in dark blue skin suits. The skin suits are shooting back with laser cannons. The bone-thin, nailed-up figure moans and bleeds, the usual morbid backdrop to this muddy melee.

Hugh sighs. He affixes his pocket amplifier, tells the time pirates that if they don't stop shooting and come quietly, they'll all be neutralized. The Romans stop hacking and stare. The pirates—the few who aren't already scattered in pieces all over Calvary—are mostly docile. Hugh quickly vaporizes the remaining Romans, along with the bits of hacked pirates and lasers, makes sure the poor skeletal man is still securely fastened to his crucifix. He seems too far gone, thank goodness, to register what's happening around him.

What did you have today? asks Polly, back at the base. She is eating sort-of-cheeseburgers, hideous gray things from the canteen that look like moldy plaster. Hugh shudders, distracted by such terrible food. He is distracted by so many things lately. I don't know how you can eat that shit, he says. Before he was a Cleaner—before the Scarcity began—he was the head chef at a fairly decent restaurant in Midtown.

Polly shrugs. I had Hitler's bunker today, she said. Everything tastes like shit after that.

Hugh doesn't blame her. Hitler's bunker is one of the worst runs. The neo-fascists shouting down the Nazi-hunters and Eva Braun's operatic screams and those fucking dogs trying to bite everybody in between. By the time the Cleaners arrive, at least dear Adolf is usually dead, but sometimes he isn't. And that's difficult, too. Because *you* try looking at that mad, paste-white face, screaming itself into a mottled beet soup, *you* try, when your great-aunt was crushed to death on a transport between Terezin and Auschwitz, only six years old and small as a toddler, *you* try to stay your hand and save that furious face for its own damned death. It takes all the effort you can muster, and sometimes, every once in a while, Hugh has arrived on the scene only to find another Cleaner standing before the lifeless body, fatally unable to resist the urge.

So Hugh can't begrudge Polly the cheeseburgers, no matter how rancid. This morning I had the Crucifixion, he said. That's never *too* bad. But this afternoon I have the Little Princes.

She looks at him sympathetically, her mouth a moue of gray gristle. They had a thing once, he and she, a few years ago. It was more of an understanding, really: after the worst of them—the Little Princes, the Children's Crusade, the Black Plague, Lidice, Nanjing—he'd spend the night at her place, nothing untoward, just hanging onto each other, really. As if the weight of all that death could be shared; as if the overflow of horror could be held, could be contained between two bodies. She finally put a stop to it—said it was just too morbid, and anyway she was planning on leaving the Cleaners soon. I'm getting old, she said. I want kids. I want to stop aging faster than everybody else around me.

Of course, you don't really leave the Cleaners. It's too hard to adjust, after, to the slow molasses of real time wrapping itself around you. It's too hard to count the seconds, the minutes, time steadily stalking forward, leaving you behind. It's hard to be the fly trapped in amber.

When the time machines were new, the public was furious they couldn't visit the future. No matter how many times the scientists patiently explained about fixed and unfixed points in time, about the instability swirling around an unfixed point, the public didn't get it. They were even angrier that they couldn't change the past. They wouldn't listen, they wouldn't follow the rules, and they planned trips to save Lincoln, to kill the slavers, to stop Rome burning and change Truman's mind about the bomb. They wanted to bring penicillin to the Plague, and artificial limbs to Civil War battlefields. They wanted to save the dodo, the rhino, the snow leopard, the honeybee, the whale. They wanted to save their loved ones, and sometimes, themselves. An astonishingly large number of them wanted to save Elvis. They planned lesser things, too, little things: revenges and romances and get-rich schemes. And so the machines were tightly secured, remained in the hands of the trained: the scientists, the military, the historians. Guided tours were given to special VIPs and reporters, to certain eras and events—but no solo trips. Of course the illicit machines sprang up anyway, badly made but worth billions, and the space pirates sprang up with them—and the Cleaners were formed to take care of these mercenaries of time.

Hugh's been a Cleaner now for ten years. It's a difficult, unrewarding job, with shitty pay and benefits. Sure, you get to See the Centuries!—like the brochure says. That's what hooked him. But all you see are the horrors of history. And all you do is stop people from stopping them. A year ago he brought the pox blankets *back* to the natives after a well-meaning group of illegal tourists stole them away. On return he had a sort of quiet breakdown. He took a month of leave, sat around eating garbage and watching TV, stared at the place in his wall where he put his fist through after his wife walked out. After they lost their little girl to the Avian Flu Pandemic. His wife had screamed and screamed at him to go back and save her, save her, but how do you save someone from a virus? There was nowhere in the folds of the world to hide, back then—the Flu was everywhere, from the biggest cities to the remotest villages. He'd almost died of it himself. His lungs have never been the same.

The Little Princes run is rougher than usual. A couple of crazy British tourists are with the pirates and they keep shouting terrible things while they're being handcuffed. They call him a child-killer. The two fair-haired little boys look on wide-eyed, too afraid and too proud to cry, and at last he lets Richard's men get on with it, training his eyes on the stone floor so he doesn't see it, though he can still hear the muffled shouts. Smothered. He'd always wondered, before this gig, and now he knows. It's not a thing he's glad to know. His daughter was blond. She was just learning how to read, and when she was stuck on a word she absently twirled her yellow curls into knots, over and over again.

Sometimes he wonders if it would really be so bad, letting people flood into history like a tidal wave and sweep away the worst of it. Sure, the paradoxes would destroy us, but so what? Did a world that let happen the Holocaust and Hiroshima and the Trail of Tears and Stalin and Genghis Khan and Pol Pot deserve to be spared? He lies on his bed for a while, the two little princes' blond heads drifting down the dark river of his brain. The terrain is more and more obscured in there; he doesn't much like where his thoughts are headed these days. Night places. Tangled and pitch-dark. He messages Polly, hoping it's still the same address.

Want to come over? he asks. The answer flashes back fast: Can't. BF's here. Sorry.

Hugh stares at the fist-sized hole in the wall. He never bothered to get it fixed after she left. He's never bothered to clean up the place, either, after the wild hurricane she became before she packed up and blew out of town. He has no idea where she is. He hopes she's okay. If he's perfectly honest with himself, it was bound to end badly; they weren't well-suited and they fought much of the time. He was never faithful to her. The only good they ever made together was the little girl.

He puts his fist into the hole, feels the sharp edges of cheap plaster crumble around it. He wishes he could push his whole body into the wall, through the wall, to somewhere outside history entirely.

At work the next day he suits up and heads to the dock. Polly is there and she touches his arm; You okay? she asks.

Fine, he says, shrugging. Just a bad night last night, that's all. I shouldn't have messaged you.

It's cool, she says. I'm around if you need to talk, okay? Just not when Pete's there—he doesn't understand. How hard it is for us, you know? It seems harder these days . . . Her voice is braided with tension, rough. He wonders.

Where you off to this morning? he asks.

Theresienstadt, she says, and frowns. A hypothermia epidemic, November '43.

Theresienstadt. The name the Germans gave to Terezin, long ago christened after the Emperor's mother. Hugh's Czechoslovakian great-aunt is still there in 1943, just shy of her sixth birthday. She acts in the little plays they put on at the camp for the Red Cross officials. She still, despite everything, loves to sing. In time, in this machine-bound stretch of time, she is still alive; it is documented, it is a fact. It is a gift.

Hey, I just have Caesar's assassination today, he says. Let me switch with you. Please?

I don't think so, Polly says, shaking her head. We could get fired.

Just tell them I stole it, then. Just tell them I made you. Tell them anything, I don't care, he says, and he's already running to her machine, he's already climbing in, he's already checking the controls, the location, the date: November 13, 1943—the Bohušovicer Kessel Census in the yard at Terezin. Polly is shouting but he's already closed the door against her face, a mouthing fish in the cold blue light of the docking bay, then gone, forgotten in the time blur, everything forgotten on the way to save the only child he can.

And now he understands the tourists. He knows, even in the blur he knows they'll come for him, they'll find her, they'll make sure she's on that cattle car in 1944. But for right now—for an hour maybe, for a minute, for just one revolution of the second hand in space—he'll have sounded a note, he'll have saved a life, he'll have wiped a stain from history before the men and women like him come and put it all to wrong once more.

Things You Should Know About Cassandra Dee

*O*ne. Cassie is an ugly girl. A rawboned, odd-angled, horsey girl. A soft, too-big jaw, drooping-eyelids, fat-under-the cheeks-that-seems-to-melt-into-the-neck girl.

Ugly people usually have at least one redeeming feature: haunting eyes, straight white teeth, perhaps a good complexion. But not Cassie. She is pale and mauve-colored, with thin brown hair and yellowy teeth—even her eyes are small. And while she isn't exactly fat, she is large, her body too wide for her head. Her ears stick out like jug handles. She is awkward, unfinished, like the bad clay sculptures kids in kindergarten make.

At school, kids call her The Lump. Her parents call her Babydoll, but they put her class pictures away in a drawer instead of hanging them in the hall with her brother's.

Two. Cassie can *See* things. Ever since she was four years old and collapsed under the tree at Aunt Betsy's Christmas party, told her mother when she came to she saw Uncle Mo's truck drive into the Platte River, and not an hour later they had a phone call from the police that there had been a bad accident and would Betsy come down and identify the body? Since then, Cassie's always been able to see things nobody else can, things that make bright flashes in her head and play like a filmstrip over her eyes. It isn't just seeing things. It's Seeing Things. She usually faints, and that for sure means that the thing she sees is important and true. Or rather, that it will be true one day. Like when she Sees the dark blue minivan is going to run over her brother's new puppy, or when she Sees her cousin Debra get her legs blown off in the desert.

The things she Sees are always death or hurt or pain. Her aunt calls it the Lord's gift, but then why did Reverend Matthews ban her from service after she Saw the grocery store fire while singing in the church choir on Sunday? He thinks it's a gift from Satan, and Cassie is inclined to agree. Especially because she knows one day she'll See her own death. And then one day she does.

It happens during Freshman Homeroom. She Sees her own body spread-eagled on a patch of grass surrounded by pink and purple flowers, big ones with wide petals. Only, it isn't quite her. It's a pretty her, a slim, shining, fair-haired copy of her. But she knows it's her just the same. And she knows it means she'll die, and soon.

She throws up on her desk and Mrs. Carver has to get the school nurse. The school and the doctors call the Sight "epilepsy," but she knows it isn't. It's a curse, that's what Cassie thinks. She's never prevented anything bad from happening. All she can do is watch.

Three. Cassie wants to be pretty, wants desperately to be pretty, would trade away the moon, the sun, and all the oceans to be pretty. Especially now that she knows she's going to die.

She hits upon the idea of plastic surgery when watching *Snow White and the Seven Dwarfs*. The idea of lying on a bleached silk cushion, Plexiglas covering the top; she would be a delicate doll figure, with small hands and feet and a beautiful face and beatific smile. Her arms would be folded and her eyes closed in rapture, like the picture of St. Catherine in her saints book. People would pass by and speak in worshipful whispers, would say how beloved she must have been—and the echo of her body would be smiling, smiling and waving like a beauty queen wherever it was you went when you died.

Her parents try to grant her wish, but all the doctors say no. The specialists, the plastic surgeons, even the celebrity doctors—they all say no. "No, no, no," they chant in unison, a Hippocratic chorus. Soon the naysayers crowd into her dreams. They stand strung together, identical and frowning and folded arms, paper-doll doctors.

Four. Cassie has blind spots, too. When she gets home from school one day, Cassie's aunt and her mother are sitting in the living room waiting for her. Her mother is smiling, and her aunt is frowning. There is a strange man with her father in the kitchen, and he is a doctor who has heard all about Cassie and has volunteered to make her pretty.

He'll do it for free, Cassie's mother says, holding out her arms to her ugly little girl. Cassie's heart explodes like trumpets, like fireworks and streamers. She's going to be beautiful. It suddenly seems okay that she'll die, now. It suddenly seems like a natural price to pay. She will be a flower, yes, a moonbeam, yes, shining briefly but bright—a silvery, shimmery memory forever.

Oh, child, says her aunt. I wish you wouldn't. Everyone loves you now. What do you need prettiness for?

Cassie says nothing. She knows she can't possibly explain. How the love people give you when you're ugly just isn't the same.

Oh, hush, says Cassie's mother. She holds Cassie to her, while her daughter cries without knowing she's crying. Her face is even uglier with the redness and the squinty eyes and tear tracks. Cassie's mother tries not to look. She was the Caton County Corn Festival Queen once, and she's still the prettiest cashier at the Safeway. Prettier than most of the other girls twenty years younger. Oh, Babydoll, won't it be nice, she murmurs into her daughter's mousy hair. Won't it be nice.

The doctor is young and good-looking, with long slender hands that will work magic on Cassie. The doctor has heard from another doctor that Cassie is going to die, and nobody exactly disabuses him of that notion. Everyone in Cassie's family believes at least a little in her Sight.

The doctor says it will take six months, and does she have that long? Cassie thinks about it, and it feels right to her. So she says yes, and the family echoes her. Yes.

Then he rolls up his metaphorical sleeves, and Cassie rolls up hers, and they get to work. He breaks her nose, puts in a chin implant, performs eyelid lifts, pins back her ears, plumps her lips up with injections, liposuctions her thighs, and gives her breast implants. It is all very painful, but Cassie has a mantra, though she doesn't know that word. I will be a moonflower, she says, over and over, when the pain gets so bad she feels she might black out. I will be a moonflower. I will.

Five. Cassie is a little in love with her doctor. This is one of her blind spots. He tells her that he will throw her a party when the bandages come off, just like Cinderella. She tries to tell him Cinderella was always pretty, but he cuts her off and smiles wider. You'll be the belle of the ball, he says.

No one has ever checked the doctor's credentials. He just

showed up on Cassie's doorstep, and the family has attributed it to Providence. If anyone had checked, they would have noticed he was no longer allowed to practice medicine. If anyone had checked, they might have seen some scary things.

Six. Cassie has always disliked mirrors. Tonight, though, she is almost dizzy at the thought of what they might reveal. Tonight, the bandages come off. And Cassie gets a haircut and highlights and her teeth whitened and even a pedicure and a manicure, and the doctor pays for it all. Tonight is the night Cassie will be reborn, briefly, before she dies. A phoenix in reverse.

Cassie puts on the dress first. It's a new silver lace froth, long and grown up, and the heels are pale pearl. She is leaving the mirror for last. She is terrified of still being ugly. The doctor's nice blue eyes widen in appreciation. You look like a beautiful fairy princess, he says. Cassie snorts—she's not a fool—but then she realizes, she might. She might be that lovely now. The thought makes her tingle and light up from head to toe, like fireflies are dancing all over her skin.

The doctor puts his hands on her bare shoulders and gently spins her around, until she's facing the full-length mirror. And then Cassie forgets all about dying, forgets about her fears and her family and everything but the floating girl before her in the glass. That's me, she whispers, and the doctor laughs. You're my very finest creation, he says. My Galatea.

He leads Cassie into the backyard, tells her the guests will be arriving soon. Will you dance with me first? he asks, and though she's never danced before, she knows she can. She's not afraid. Not even when the doctor puts his arm around her waist, and her breath catches. She ignores the strange warmth in her blood and concentrates on stepping in the right places. She's so beautiful, she realizes, is it any wonder he would want to dance with her?

And as they dance he starts to sing to her, softly, Oh, you must have been a beautiful baby, you must have been a wonderful child . . .

Cassie smiles to think of her own history rewritten. She looks down, shy in her new skin now, and sees her pearl shoes sink into a green patch of grass, edged by pink and purple flowers. Big flowers. Her vision goes black for a moment, then as her sight ebbs back in waves she looks up, really looks, right into the doctor's nice blue eyes. They have gone soft, unfocused, pupils wide, and she sees her new pretty face reflected in the empty blackness.

And she doesn't *See* it but she sees it just the same: her mother weeping prettily beside a casket with pink and beige insides, her aunt's head bent in sad disapproval. Her cousins shifting, uneasy at the funeral, uncomfortable and bored in stiff black suits and ties. Her class, politely shuffling by at the wake, puzzled by what they suppose are the wonders of mortuary makeup. She looks better dead, an unkind classmate will whisper, and Cassie's father will clench his fists and plant his huge, useless bulk on the front pew because what else, whatever else can he do?

But now she twists away, she tries to run, shedding one shoe; but the doctor catches her hard by the wrist and throws her to the ground. Please don't hurt me, she says, but she knows he will hurt her, hurt her so badly she will never get up again. She's been resigned to her death, but now that she knows how she'll die it seems wrong, it seems bad and unfair and a cheat. And so she cries for the beautiful little girl she had living inside of her all along, like a wood spirit trapped in a tree.

Seven. Cassie can no longer See, and she sobs and sobs as the man kneels stiffly down beside her to whisper the rest of his song in her pinned-back ear. You must have been a beautiful *bay-ay-bee,* he sings softly, his fingers long and slender and working fast. She opens. She closes. She is a single flower, born and then gone under the silver strands of moonlight.

The Fires of Western Heaven

Sandbags rim the mouth of the trench, swarmed by tangles of barbed wire. The sentries lie here and there with their periscopes, improving their loopholes, bolstered by the approach of dawn. You climb the fire steps and look through the early morning mists, silvering the white and chalky soil. The dreams of the dead seem to swim through the shadows of No Man's Land, just past what you can see. There is almost nothing to mark the horizon: farms, churches, landmarks—even the ruins have been ruined, pounded into oblivion by the constant shelling. One small cottage is all that remains of the broken village past the field, just bits of plaster and a wall.

❦

Sometimes the blackness descends, months and years later, and we find ourselves back there again. We are floating above the earth, or no, we *are* the earth, we are grass and trees, we are England and Germany, we are the Italian Alps and the Turkish Dardanelles, we are boys and girls, parents and grandparents, sorrow and anger and joy and bitter, bitter hearts. It is a very strange way to see, through the *all* of it, and it feels heavy as a blanket made of iron. We are riding in a dense, dark wood. We ride with the dead and with the living. We ride hard the hounds and show no mercy to the fox.

We ride hard to forget, but the dead ride with us.

◆

Edmund, drowned in the mud at Passchendaele. Stuck and sinking for twenty minutes, while his helpless lieutenant watched him go.

Lettie, dead of the Spanish flu, carried by a cargo of sailors to her port town. Her small sisters followed, one by one by one.

All the Giordano boys, fallen in France, and not one proper grave between them.

Blair, gassed at the first Ypres, kept his life but lost his sight and lungs and laugh. Lost the color in his hair and face.

Mrs. Winthrop's old husband, the Major, sunk off the coast of Africa.

Katarina, finished with food after she lost Paul. She wouldn't eat, she wouldn't eat, and eventually she grew so thin she wore wool in high summer. And then she wore nothing at all, and the land claimed her little white bones.

◆

Soon the night patrols will come back, the sentries will stand down, and the men will start exchanging insults and songs with the soldiers across the bombed-out No Man's Land. In broken French and broken German and a little broken English, they'll swap opinions on the local estaminet—the beer is swill, the eggs rotten, the chips just edible—and on which French women to bed and which to avoid. There'll be a few jokes about that, too, and calls for names, names, please, because after all the VD will land an infantryman in the hospital just as well as a piece of shrapnel.

After the Stand-To, then inspection, then rum with breakfast on this chilly morning. The men will gather at the largest shell hole to wash and shave, cheerfully saying good morning to their dead German soldier as they file past. They inherited Fritz, as they call him, when they arrived a few days ago, and they've been watching him turn colors ever since. White then yellow then red then blue, and now he's got a greenish cast. There are bets on when the black will set in, though they all hope they're back behind the lines before then. The panic and boom of the Salient will sound in the distance soon, too. The rat hunting will begin in earnest, rodent corpses strung like grotesque necklaces over the trench throats. The whole jagged mess of war and life will make a sharp wound against the brightness once more.

❦

Tom, the happy warrior, shot in the neck while leading a charge. It took him four days to die. He called out for his mother but the veil came first.

When Valentina's brother died in the Alps, she shipped out as a nurse to France and her father died of grief a month later.

When the Carthaginians made sacrifice, they played loud music near the fires so no one could hear the little children screaming. Said Georges to everyone when he returned from Siberia.

Davis, mad in a quiet way; he sat alone on park benches and wept.

Mary needed a false set of teeth but there were none left—they'd all gone to the soldiers. She ate oatmeal and mashed potatoes for years while dreaming of bacon.

Rory's face, blown off in Sardinia. The doctors gave him a new

123

one. It was called a great miracle. Either it broke all the mirrors or he did.

❖

Sometimes we find a little of what has been lost. Sometimes it is a comfort, sometimes a nightmare. Sometimes it is a mystery, a thing so far removed from now it appears like an alien artifact, singing in the wild of unimaginable kindnesses. These things are written in a language we no longer need, that we no longer believe in. Pages with dog-eared corners, letters dressed with pieces of ribbon and lace, pressed leaves and flowers from earlier walks through woods. Souvenirs of another kind of silence.

Now we spill down through the forest, now we ride into human crowds and there are fevers for us, wild jazz and absinthe dreams, garters and girdles and stockings rolled down. Raucous piano and jitterbugging and casual sex in the park, in the plaza, in the piazza, in the backseat of the Rolls. Everywhere there is fever and passion, everywhere a need to burn, burn, burn out the hurt. We write, we sing, we paint, and still the blackness follows, still the dead are there in every note, every brushstroke. We ride and ride, farther and faster and still, still the ghosts ride with us, keep pace behind us, mock all our efforts to smoke and sweat them out.

❖

Now the inky sky and the stiff-armed sentries and the breathing of sleepers further down the trench. Uneasy, shallow sleep, made restless with wounds real or imagined. Night here has a way of spreading fear like a contagion, making men who hate violence long for the sudden rough burst of it. Something decisive, something solid, something other than this half-life of sickness and waiting. Most of the men are sick with something: trench foot, dysentery, flu, fever. Fear. Nightmares. A trench full of sick men breathing in hope and dreaming about home. The cleanse before dawn. Before they wake tired and sore, remembering the bombardment starts today. The relentless sound of the artillery guns their only music for the next week. The air they breathe will hum and vibrate with it; the light itself will bend and waver and blacken with the endless shower of shells. Then they'll explode the mines, finally, take out the Boche guns, then rush their lines. After the attack, they're going behind the lines again, what's left of the company, of course. Once the relief comes.

◆

Delia, married to a steel magnate who made a killing off of the war. But she secretly went to the toilet every night and cried for a boy buried in Flanders.

Danny, the poet, devoid of poetry now. Instead of words he dreams of cave-ins and close fights in a tunnel of earth and water.

◆

All the pictures flung past, the living only half of what's missing. If you look closely, you can just make out the outlines of the dead peering over our shoulders, as we dance, as we sing carols, as we mark the holidays off with ticks on a calendar and births and deaths in Bibles. As we ride, ride, these woods are full of the gloom of the ghostly riders behind us. As we ride, and years wear on, these ghosts never change, never age, always stare glumly at the camera, as green and ungainly as they were at twenty-one. These riders still burn with the fire of the western heavens.

◆

Davy, gassed, drowned on dry land. His nightmare face stuck in his mates' minds for years, green and gasping, eyes rolling and red like a dying bull's.

Jack, pulverized in the heat of the Dardanelles, nothing left to ship home.

Roland, shot for mutiny. By then glad to know how he was going to die, and that it would be clean, and painless, and quick.

Jürgen, fallen from the sky like Icarus. Not in a firefight; his plane developed engine trouble and he went down in front of a clear, bright blue sky and a burning sun.

◆

In the end, nothing left but the trees; twisted things whittled by shrapnel and fire to pointed black stakes. They hold up the sky and fence in the killing fields, make a hideous trinket of barbed wire and wood.

In the end, take the photos of past school classes and strike them through: an *X*, an *X*, an *X*, an *X*.

In the end, the battle-scarred world stands still.

The Process of Human Decay

Fresh

Something is wrong. Your heart, it seems, has become a fish. It leaps, flutters, flops sideways a few times, then stops. You fall down.

Just an hour ago your muscles were loose and limber and you walked down the street to the neighbor's, stood on his stoop and talked about your grandkids, spring training, gas prices. Now your thighs and calves are tightening, rigid, blood pooling under the skin. Your brain cells are losing their structural integrity. Putrefaction has started, and the carbohydrates and lipids have begun to form gases in your intestinal tract. An army of blowflies is already on the way.

Bloat

Your daughter stands nervously behind the cops as they force open your door. This is harder than it looks with you sprawled in the door-way, heavy with decay. The smell bursts from the front hallway and everyone gasps, even your daughter. After only five days it seems impossible she wouldn't recognize you, but you are not you. You have transmogrified; you are a monster, a shiny human skin sack stuffed with liquefying tissue, leaking from every orifice.

The smell of it all is unbearable and one of the cops mutters something about masks. Your daughter, made brave by grief, puts her T-shirt over her mouth and tries to get closer. It is then that your skin begins to ripple and marble. She runs from the house, and it isn't the first time. You have been a grotesque to her while living, even as you were to her mother before her. Your current state of gracelessness reminds us now that you have not always lived with grace. Though in the last few years you have tried to atone, there is a reason you have lived alone often. There is a reason several wives have wished you would die—and finally you have.

Delayed Decay

You wanted to be cremated; you told your daughter and your son and your sisters and your wretched almost-ex-wife. But somehow, no one has listened. They just want to throw you in a box and bury you as quickly as they can.

Your almost-ex-wife says a few words that aren't true, and your daughter tries but just keeps crying, something her grown children have never seen her do. Their uncle cries, but that's nothing new. He always was a pussy, your son. Your grandkids, though—two boys, good kids—they play baseball for their college teams and they date pretty girls. You think one of them might be a Mormon. You disapprove of God, but you had still hoped to become a better man for their sake. You hoped to show them how to stay men, unlike their uncle. You would be sad to see how little they seem to mind your passing. They look dismayed but mostly distracted, hot and itchy in black wool on a warm spring day. Get it over with, they seem to be saying, and you would probably agree. You were never one for ceremony. Get it over with, and here comes the lid and the shovel and the earthy hole. Here come the worms.

Dry Remains

Eventually decomposition strips you bare, even in that solid oak you've taken the shape of. You've helped, finally, to enrich something around you, by feeding the soil with your skin and fat and muscle. Now the soil is full of phosphorus, potassium, calcium, and especially nitrogen. Now the soil is supremely satisfied, and you'd be okay with that. You always did like growing things. You always were better with plants than with people.

The Fever Librarian

Some days are harder than others for the fever librarian. Some days, the sadness freezes in her veins, and on these still days she is able to file and sort, to restock and research and perform her duties as she always has. But some days, the ice breaks up and the memory ships can navigate through, laden with their dangerous cargo: lust, anger, obsession. On these days her fingers itch to release all the fevers, to bring back all of man's carnal passions and searing pains. To spread illness and abandon throughout the known world.

The fever librarian is keeping it quiet, but an epidemic has begun to infect her heart; it is spreading through her brain and body like wildfire. Her irises are blackening, her hair is darkening to copper, her skin is just starting to betray the red of the fevers burning inside of her.

From the Eternal Library's Official Employee Handbook: *The brain of the Fever Librarian should be made mostly of melancholy. The Fever Librarian should wear black bile in the veins. The Fever Librarian should be an unmarried woman with a soft, drowned heart, and a choleric disposition. She should be pale and thin, with a look that hints at Perpetual Anguish of the Soul. She should resemble someone's grandmother, someone we have known for ages in the abstract. Dependable. Invisible.*

From the Eternal Library's Official Employee Handbook: *One would do better to forget the Fever Librarian's name as soon as one has learned it. She would do better to forget her own.*

—

The opposite of melancholy is fierce, bright delirium. It has a name: fever, also known as pyrexia, comes from the Greek *pyr*, meaning *fire*.

The fever librarian has read all the scholarship, has attended the debates and listened to the shouted discussion on the radio programs. Some scholars are furious at the fevers being catalogued and contained. These scholars say the fevers are a good, or at least a necessary evil, humanity's way of fighting illness and tedium. We once prayed they did not last long, and endured the irrationality they engendered, and we breathed a long slow breath of relief when they had gone. And now humanity, these scholars claim, is scarcely human at all. We move like molasses, they say, in this mire of supreme rationality. We are barely beings, so calculating and calm are we.

The scholars on the other side argue, of course, that man lives in a golden age of enlightenment. Now, they say, we have the mental reserves and energy to study and dream up great improvements for the human race. Now, they say, we have rid the body of wasteful passions and useless energies expended, hours stolen from every day to relieve our unspeakable animal urges. We are more human than ever, these scholars say; we have finally risen above our shameful pasts, more than angels, we, with each new experiment.

❖

The fever librarian comes from a time of incredible yearning. Plucked from the past, deprived of memory, she still retains certain physical imprints of that time. Her body remembers dancing, and driving, and craning the neck to take in great tall buildings going up at greater speeds. Her body remembers fear, too, and pain, and the way her limbs had of leaving her control for the refuge of a neck or a chest or another pair of lips—unthinkable, the idea of violating the space of another human body, but as her veins thaw and her skin warms, these memories begin to surface as she moves, as she walks and rises and sits and stands and even as she breathes.

When the Eternal Librarians chose her, they sealed all things past in a great ice heart, frozen inside her for all of time. This is always the way the Librarians are created, and contained. This is the way the world's memory is kept safe. But the Eternal Librarians did not understand the far-reaching effects of the fevers. They did not understand what such heat could do to an ice heart.

And so the fever librarian sleeps a great deal now, for only in sleep can she find relief from all the human passions caged in her four chambers. And so the fever librarian spends a great deal of time studying herself in mirrors, fearful of giving anything away. She is trying very hard to be invisible, tepid and faint as an early morning shadow. But she watches with awe and fear as the hair reddens, the skin reddens, as the eyes betray the rising temperature of the body underneath them. She watches and she worries she will soon be found out. She worries she will soon be overtaken.

❖

Pliny the Elder estimated the number of human illnesses at three hundred, but of course assented that no one really knew the full range. He believed fever an illness, like most learned men of his time, and suggested, among other remedies, wine for shoring up good health and preventing disease. His favorite brew contained spikenard, cardamom, cinnamon, saffron, and ginger. The truth, he said, comes out in wine.

There is no wine in the Eternal Library. Wine warms unforgivably; truths breed euphoria and inevitably, passion. The preferred drink now is a weak tea brewed faintly with calming herbs like lavender and chamomile, cooled and drunk at room temperature. From the Eternal Library's Official Employee Handbook: *The Librarian's preferred draft should be the heady nectar of a day's careful research. External foods and beverages are necessary only to sustain the inner studies, and should never be enjoyed or sought out during working hours. Such seeking could prove dangerous to the Librarian and indeed, to the efficient functioning of the Library itself.*

There are only working hours for the fever librarian. These triple-lined, carefully cooled cabinets are full of all the fevers man and god could dream up: alchemy, Cat-Scratch Fever, Congo Hemorrhagic Fever, goldfish swallowing, Dr. Spock, Trench Fever. Acid wash, chariot racing, ant farms, holy wars, hula hoops, Humidifier Fever, monkeys on television. Jumping beans, Beatniks, ballooning, Rocky Mountain Spotted Fever, the Orient, witch mania, cockfighting, Maternal Fever, table-rapping, drag racing, Pac Man, Parrot Fever, Metal Fume Fever, dance marathons, self-flagellation, African Hemorrhage Fever, the Crusades, Typhoid Fever, quiz shows, Lassa Fever, Rubix Cube, phone booth stuffing, toga parties, Scarlet Fever, Septic Fever, Swamp Fever, water beds, zoot suits, trading cards, competitive sports, Autumn Fever, spring fever, beach movies, chivalry, secret orders, grail quests. Little Lord Fauntleroy. Dream fever. Sexual fever.

Love.

The Egyptians recognized that local inflammation was responsible for fever. They observed that the pulse would accelerate under its influence.

Throughout history, it was assumed that fever gave either divine or devilish powers to the possessor, or rather, the possessed. In some cases, the fevered person was observed in acts of prophecy; the fevered person related fantastic visions that had come to them in this heightened state. In other cases, the fevered person was seized by demons and flung about the room, or made to spout unintelligible gibberish, or commit violence upon themselves or others. In some cases, the fevered person was given to fits of sexual passion and mania, and opinion differed in these cases as to whether demonic or angelic possession was at work in the human flesh.

The Mesopotamians believed that only evil spirits brought fever, and that only under the priests' cool influence could it be exorcised from the body. There were no exceptions, for the side of good could never be the side of the flame.

❧

As of late, the fever librarian dislikes the days she is asked to be grateful for facts, to applaud their long-term stability, their rigid domesticity. The fever librarian has tried to explain about the mutability and unreliability of facts on a very long timeline. Facts, she says, exist for ages—whole lifetimes, centuries, epochs—and then they disappear into the wretched night of ignorance and myth.

The fever librarian is increasingly unwilling to rely on the hardwood floor of facts as a foundation. She is increasingly unwilling to ignore the rot that eventually sets in anywhere, in any seemingly sturdy floor. She is increasingly unwilling to sit here, day in and day out, no love, no conversation, no apartment to call home. No dreams but those locked in this thawing ice heart.

This is not to say that the fever librarian is not a very good steward of facts, just the same. She is vigilant and organized. Her notebooks and memories and databases are full of all the world's facts, the passions of every age etched in permanent slashes and dots over the membranes and folds. The fever librarian does not forget. The facts are always at her fingertips, whether the subject is fallout shelters or conical bras or the swift speed at which the bubonic fever strikes. The fever librarian remembers everything. She remembers the danger, especially; all human sickness and folly is her waking, worrisome dream.

❦

The rooms in which the fevers are stored must be cool and dark and quiet to keep the fevers from stray sparks, from reignition. The fever librarian has, as a result, spent a lifetime as silent as a Benedictine monk. Forget conversation or music; even the sun is not allowed to shine aloud in these halls. As of late, the fever librarian has felt isolated, has felt lonely, has felt the walls not closing in but expanding, spreading, growing the silent darkness into a massive, arctic sort of prison.

When she first began to work in these rooms, many eons ago, she was assured that the Librarians were solitary creatures, meant to work alone in a kind of devotion, a worship of knowledge and learning. As of late, she is not so sure of this. As of late, the fever librarian is starting to hunger for the touch, the smell, the weight of another human body. She is starting to feel a little mad.

⬥

The Greeks divided fever into four categories: continuous, from excess of fire; intermittent, due to excess of water; quotidian, from excess of air; and quartan, caused by an excess of earth. They also believed most fevers were fed by an excess of yellow bile. The patients infected were starved and given honey with water, or hydromel, to reduce the bile and blood in the body.

Arab doctors in the Middle Ages were vastly more knowledgeable about fevers than their European counterparts. Abu Bakr ibn Muhammad Zakariya al-Razi, a great scholar and philosopher, was the first to distinguish between the two terms "fever" versus "hyperthermia" in the form of heatstroke. Fever caused by the sun. The Eternal Library is careful to prevent both types.

In the nineteenth century, fever was still regarded as its own separate disease, and indeed a disease with many variants and causes. Autumnal fever, jail fever, hospital fever, bilious fever, nervous fever, malignant and even pestilential fever were all supposed separate forms of this disease.

Also in the nineteenth century, Charles Mackay wrote that "men, it has been well said, think in herds; it will be seen that they go mad in herds, while they only recover their senses slowly, and one by one."

He wrote: "How flattering to the pride of man to think that the stars on their courses watch over him, and typify, by their movements and aspects, the joys or the sorrows that await him!"

The Eternal Library does not acknowledge a heaven. The Eternal Library's official policy states: *Man is life's custodian. The Librarians are the custodians of man and his passions, and any knowledge he conceives of or possesses.* Therefore, the librarians are the custodians of the stars and the skies; any other notion of heaven is a dream, a false idol to explain the fall of mankind.

❖

William Osler once said that humanity has three enemies: "fever, famine, and war, but fever is by far the greatest."

The Eternal Library firmly agrees. This is why they must lock up the fevers, with all the spells and science and strength of will that lives in the world. This is why the fever librarian must never fail. The consequences would be unthinkable—an unending disaster for the future of man.

❖

Sometimes, the fever librarian wonders if she might be her own ghost. She cannot be sure of how long she has been here at the Eternal Library. She cannot be sure that she still has a soul. Her heart beats, her skin burns and bleeds, but a ghost, too, can be full of blood. A ghost can be a billion years old and dead inside forever.

Only this ghost feels sure she is rising from the dead at last. She is not sure of anything else in the world, of the facts or the fevers or the future, but she is sure that a thing is about to begin or end; which, she does not know.

❖

It is late in the year, the season of bonfires, when the fevers finally swarm and overtake the librarian that tends them. She has been smoldering for months under their disturbing influence. Now she begins to burn.

Be assured that the fever librarian is actually the hero of her story. Be assured that she is much stronger than she looks, especially in the throes of such heart-driving heat. Here she is eating her notes. Here she is pulling out drawer after drawer of index cards. Here she is overturning the tables in this temple of learning. Here she is with gallons, with buckets, with fire hoses of water to put out these fevers and drown all our passions and finally, finally send them back to the sea from whence all our troubles are come.

The Unfinished World

S et swam into the world with the new century. He was so many years the youngest that he sat as audience for his siblings, rapt in the soft glow of their stage presence. And in return they made him their favorite. They protected him; they enfolded him in their obsessions; they gave him their secrets to keep.

His brother Cedric, an explorer by trade, took him to dusty, dark museums fallen out of favor. He showed Set impossibly large-hipped stone women and spear tips and tiny skulls no bigger than an apple. He told Set stories about the hunter that brought down the saber-tooth, about the pygmy races who lived hidden in the hearts of jungles, about the sleep spells shamans cast in the days before dreams were invented.

Constance—his only sister—served him sweets and ginger beer, and bought him penny dreadfuls and souvenir pen wipers—all the things his mother, Pru, forbade for their vulgarity. (Pru did not quite say that Constance was vulgar, though she labeled her "modern" in a way that implied no small degree of disappointment.) Constance liked to read Set love letters from her admirers.

She would laugh, a low laugh like far-off thunder, and toss the letters on the fire. They always seemed to be from glamorous people. Set ambushed a distracted Pru at the piano one afternoon and asked if his sister was famous, and Pru frowned and said, yes, possibly more than she should have been. Set asked what she was famous *for*, and the Chopin became very loud indeed.

Set's father was the family enigma. He died when Set was quite small, and before that he did not seem to live in the big house on Long Island with Pru and Cedric and Constance and Oliver. He was always just Father, a blur or blank half-remembered, filled with whiskers and ample pocket-watch chain, large teeth and small keen eyes. In later years, Set was always mixing up his memories of Father and of President Roosevelt on newsreel.

Set's brother Oliver had an orderly mind, doors for each feeling and shelves for the strongest memories. So it was not surprising to Set that Oliver should own a self-dubbed Cabinet of Curiosities that he opened only for Set and for his lover, Desmond, whom everyone pretended was Oliver's business partner even though he and Oliver used to sit in the back at the Fortuna Music Hall and do what Set-as-a-child thought was a good deal of embracing for two grown men with whiskers.

Pru allowed Oliver to keep his cabinet in the parlor: a long room clad in green and garnet, full of model ships and music boxes and stuffed owls, it was the perfect place for Oliver's oddities. Oliver said his cabinet contained the best of this world and the remnants of the one before it. Set was confused and fascinated by it, this gilded wooden case, long as one wall and topped in sections by a carved snake, a wolf, and a fierce giantess; this exhibit where brass clocks butted against stringless lutes, and chalky human bones overlapped pearlescent fish scales and fetuses floating in jars. Indonesian ceremonial masks jostled for space with small paintings by Manet and Matisse and Toulouse-Lautrec; a little glass chimera peeked out from behind a magic lantern; leather pouches full of old faerie dust sat squat and useless, their magical essence long since dried up; three crystal balls were wrapped in maps made by Chinese explorers in the 1500s; a tapestry of a stag hunted by dogs hung crooked and slashed in one corner; a jar full of trolls' feet was tipped over and spilling out; and everywhere were stuffed creatures, claws and feathers, obelisks, pieces of armor, bits of Claude Lorrain glass, and branches made of wood, of iron, of ash.

It's just a jumble, Set said to Oliver, the first time he was allowed to view the collection. He preferred the museums Cedric took him to, the glass cabinets and typed cards serving as careful descriptors. Those objects felt old, felt important. They were discoveries. What was all this except a lot of disordered rubbish?

Oliver and Desmond smiled at one another. There *is* an order, said Oliver. You just need the key. He showed Set the thick black notebook—the Catalogue, he called it, and Set had the uncanny sense that this was Oliver's brain, the flesh made word—filled with precise descriptions and locations for each item in the collection in Oliver's small, careful handwriting. *Curiosity #21*, read Set. *Preserved* Chlamyphorus truncatus, *commonly known as the pink fairy armadillo. Specimen originally from central Argentina, acquired 1890.* He flipped to the middle of the notebook: *Curiosity #760. Hinged brass collar, Iron Age. Embellished with decorative patterns in the Celtic style. Inlaid with glass or precious stones; ornaments missing or lost.*

Inge was born as her mother died. She grew to resemble her mother so much that her father despised her; he saw her as a constant reminder of all he had lost. He had doted on her sisters and brother, had been a fair, if slightly stern father. But now he abandoned the care of his youngest to her exceedingly English governess: a stout woman with a wine-colored complexion and a faint brown mustache, a woman who went in for pinching and hair pulling and other invisible injuries. Inge's older siblings were sent to boarding school, but Inge was not. (The family had also, it should be said, fallen into penury by then.) Your father, said the governess, has thrown you away, and she would squeeze the soft underside of Inge's arm, or, when she was impassioned into imprudence, smack Inge across the mouth so hard that her lip split. On those occasions, Inge was instructed to spin tales of her own clumsiness, and these only served to make her father dislike her more. Her mother, the mirror, had been so graceful. The older she grew, the less her father could bear to look at her. And so, as the money dried up and the decaying manor fell apart around them—and the family and few remaining servants moved into a single wing—still Inge's father managed to avoid her, dining late and rising early, spending days walking with his dogs and his rifle out in the village and through the abandoned tenant farms.

Like many lonely children, Inge retreated into a life of the mind. Her family still had a grand library, damp in the winter from the leaking roof but gloriously full of books. She read voraciously. She liked the plays best: the Greek tragedies, Shakespeare's histories, Molière's farces. Her tutor Mr. Trimble, a dapper little man straight from Dickens, taught her to read Latin and French, and she devoured the books of Hugo and Flaubert. She read Melville's *Typee* and dreamed of adventures on the South Seas. And when she was quite old, perhaps twelve or thirteen, Mr. Trimble discovered she had read no faerie stories (for their library contained none) and brought her the whole of George MacDonald's collected tales. The mustachioed governess disapproved. She did not believe little girls should be taught untrue things; that such lessons would take root in the mind and cause appalling flights of fancy. But Mr. Trimble kept the books in his rented room in town, and brought Inge a steady supply. She thought *At the Back of the North Wind* was the loveliest book she had ever read, and she vowed that someday she, too, would leave her lonely home and her small village and her cold, distant family, and that she, too, would ride the wind, right up to those little islands in the sun-soaked parts of the world. And she thought she might take Mr. Trimble with her—even though he was older than her father, and rather crumple-faced and pockmarked—because he understood that the most important things in the world were the kind you made up for yourself. And also because he wouldn't take up very much room in the boat.

❧

Photograph: Snapshot of a telegram, rain-smeared, ink-run, and largely illegible. Crumpled and torn and missing corners, yellowed not from age but from handling.

❧

The first demon Inge buried was Albert, though he never would stay under for good. It was just like him; he was as stubborn and vain as she was. And so aside from books, floating over the sea and the rivers and the island streams, even under the great heart-eating love of Set—there was always and always Albert. She remembered trailing her older brother everywhere when he was home on holiday, begging him to teach her to shoot pheasant when she was just six. She remembered how she learned about their mother from him: that she was blond and fond of blue, like Inge; that she was beautiful and tone-deaf; that despite her brilliance, her English was always a little broken. Inge remembered Albert teaching her a mouthful of the German he'd learned from their mother. *Bitte und danke. Gern geschehen.*

She remembered how her older sisters, when home from school, would mock and mimic the way the youngest child trailed the oldest. She remembered their lace frocks and airs, the rich boys from Belfast they spoke of, the cold eyes they rolled at her as she sat with a book before the fire. Changeling, they called her, and they told her she was a faerie child, switched at birth for their real sister. But they never dared torment Inge in front of Albert. They knew he would, as he often threatened, slap the smirks off their silly faces.

Inge remembered agreeing to let Albert read her all of Kipling's *Jungle* stories, even though she'd already read them many times by herself. She remembered sewing her own suffragette sash, greeting him at the door when the car brought him back from Trinity one gray winter day. He'd told her all about his pretty girlfriend, how she wouldn't marry until women had the vote. Inge remembered being angry. How dare this woman deny her *Bruder* anything? She would be a better suffragette than his girlfriend; she would cook him dinner and bring him his slippers every evening, she told him. She remembered her shame when he laughed at her, and her relief, complicated and fierce, when he told her he would always love her best of all.

And she remembered when the family stood outside in the

rain and waited as the boy on the bicycle pedaled slowly up the winding road through the fields from the village. They watched him with agonizing stillness, a boy growing from a pinprick to a person. She remembered how he finally stopped in front of the manor. How they held their breath and watched his hands, those terrible child's hands, bringing them a piece of paper they could never be rid of. She remembered her father's face, gone paler than the paper. And she remembered thinking, ashamed of the thought even as it surfaced: Now I have no one at all.

◆

Curiosity #7: Adult American grizzly bear's left incisor, circa 1904. Removed after death.

◆

The first thing Set remembered in his own short life was the bear. Of course, "remember" is a tricky term; rather, he *thought* about the bear—the huge hungriness of it, the small black eyes, the limp, lank fur, the almost leisurely way it was loping toward him—in the kind of piled-up, fuzzy, impressionistic way the young mind has of cataloguing things. The bear, he was later told, was part of a visiting circus from Hamburg; its unfortunate name was Bumbles and it was trained to stand on its hind legs and eat dangled fish. But Set did not remember any of this: not the bright, garish colors of the circus tent, nor the off-key organ music, nor the screams of the other children as the bear, starved and beaten, tore its trainer's arm off before turning to the plumper, less threatening residents of the surrounding stands. Set remembered only the bear itself emerging, a god from the void, and the scarlet pain of the huge jaws on his head, the clutch, the clamping, viselike; then the jet of red, the small black eye exploding backward, the furious roar, the heavy sudden slump of fur. He remembered, then, how Cedric holstered his gun and how he rose in the melee, throwing Set over his huge shoulder like a sack of flour. He remembered growing cold, and wondering why, and wondering also that any human, even Cedric, could stop a thing so large, and he remembered a sense of sadness, too, that a thing so large could be dead. He remembered Cedric's frantic, half-mouthed exhortations to some god or other, layered over the low moans of horror from the circus crowds. He remembered nothing more, then, for a long while after.

◆

Curiosity #17: Heavy cavalry officer's saber, circa 1821. Used by British lieutenant during the Second Boer War; periodic sharpening, indicating a bloodied blade.

◆

After the bear, Set sensed that everything had changed, though he didn't know quite why. He woke gradually to these strange new days, feeling almost nothing at first, remembering almost nothing at all. There was a cave just behind his breastbone; it was a drafty, dark place he would come to think of as his hollow. And his family hovered. Other things, too, were different: people seemed smaller, and when they spoke their voices seemed to come from somewhere very far away. There seemed almost a hush hanging over his home. Set became slowly accustomed to these differences, and he learned to mask his feelings, his perceptions about the world. He learned a new kind of smile for when there was nothing to smile about. He became inwardly solemn and outwardly placid, by all appearances an ordinary little boy.

It was decided that Set needed a holiday, so Cedric took him on the train to the World's Fair in St. Louis. It was a marvelous dream for a small boy, and Set was enchanted from the first glimpse of the plaster-of-Paris Roman baths. Everything was massive; everything was built to scale for the gods. There was an enormous birdcage, a temple carved of teak, a vast Ferris wheel, great iron and stone statues lining the boulevards, and—Set's favorite wonder—a huge organ, the largest in the world, where the famous French organist Alexandre Guilmant played recitals every day from memory. There were hundreds of exotic animals: tiny elephants and limber orangutans, big cats with snow-white fur, and sinuous, deadly snakes. And there were exotic people, too: from new territories like Guam, Puerto Rico, and the Philippines, and native peoples from the wilder parts of the American West. There were whole South African villages, filled with men and ladies wearing nothing but underclothes. There were Alaskan tribes with their own icehouses, Pacific peoples with totem poles and canoes. Shamans from Africa made great displays of making the old young again. Some sold shrunken heads. There was even a real live pygmy from the Congo, and Set was enchanted at his acrobatics, though Cedric complained that they exploited him shamefully. Set was reminded of nothing so much as Oliver's cabinet at home, each pavilion jammed full of mystery and riddle. Secret magic in every corner.

They attended what was billed as the greatest military spectacle in the history of the world—a reenactment of the Second Boer War—played out in an enormous, fifteen-acre arena. The whole battle took three hours and Set sat breathless until the final act, when the famous Boer General Christiaan de Wet "escaped" by diving thirty-five feet on horseback into a pool of water. After, Set was very tired and could hardly keep his eyes open as Cedric dragged him to the Japanese Pavilion. Which might explain why she seemed so indistinct, so soft and dreamlike, the pretty Japanese lady in the red silk kimono. She knelt so they were face to face.

You're different, she said quietly. Aren't you? You have a different kind of life inside you.

Set was speechless. What did this lady mean?

My grandfather was special like this, she said, and smiled. You are, too. I can tell. You are friendly with the spirits.

The lady had the blackest, straightest hair he had ever seen, and her skin shone like the surface of the moon. Her voice was so light, so musical, that it drove all thoughts of dashing soldiers and horseback and deeds of glory right out of his head. He didn't know what she meant, but he would keep her words in his head like a lovely tune. He would keep them secret, his own small mystery to savor.

Before he left for France, Albert brought Inge a book of poems by Hopkins. Trust in goodness, he told her, cheerful as ever, sure of himself. The first and the last siblings stood together, bookends of a closed family dynasty. Dark and light, tall and short, thin and plump. But they both had the same open, cheerful face, the same honest blue eyes, the same love for one another.

Is the world a good place, Albert? she asked. She wasn't sure.

It didn't seem, from her bleak vantage point here in the damp and the cold and the lonely, that it was.

I think so, said Albert. But don't take my word for it, love. Go see for yourself. Go and find out what the world is.

And if you die? She swallowed the last word but still it came out a little, choked and cold.

Albert bent down, took her small hands. If I die, he said gravely, I'm still here. Aren't I? All the things I am now, they'll still be here, right? I'll never leave you, not really.

She wondered then, if *anyone* really left you. Was the world crowded with ghosts? Was that the point of suffering: to understand, in some way, what you still had? To clarify it, to own it, to rip the stars from the sky and hold them in the hand like diamonds— to darken all the rest but the most glittering, glad memories? Was that the way to live a sunny life?

❧

Curiosity #36: Square coin made of beaten gold, imprinted with a woman's image. She holds both spear and shield.

❧

For a long time after the bear, Set would wake with the feeling he'd forgotten something. He had strange dreams that felt like memories, like lost bits of other lives. For a long time after, before he got used to this hollow in himself, he would scream, would cry, would babble garbled dream descriptions to Pru: always such ordinary things like sailing or swimming or catching fireflies in jars, and yet they had the quality of nightmare because they seemed attached to someone else entirely. Pru told him not to worry. She told him he was different; she said he had lived another life and that he might remember it in sleep.

Am I a spirit? he asked.

Pru pursed her lips and shook her head. No, she said. You're my son. And she refused to discuss it further. In time he grew used to the visions, but never to the sick feeling they gave him. He often woke, weak and drained, feeling he'd survived a small death.

At such moments, it was up to Cedric and Oliver to distract Set properly. Set would have liked to play with the children who lived on neighboring estates, some of whom were his own age. But Pru forbade it. He didn't even attend school; instead Set had a series of tutors, an interchangeable set of dreary, dry men. He desperately wanted to attend school, to play sports, to join clubs. But Pru said he was special, fragile, and only his family would be able to protect him. Only your family can know you, she said, over and over, and Set had no idea what she meant but he usually sighed and settled for Cedric's chatter or Oliver's quiet company then.

Cedric liked to talk of gods and monsters; he spun tales for Set of what shaped the world eons ago, before man sailed its oceans and scaled its peaks. When Set was very small, Cedric told him about the last god to leave the earth. Once, said Cedric, there was a golden age, and men and gods lived peacefully together. There was great abundance of food and drink, and men lived long and wanted for nothing. The gods ruled well, and man in turn was obedient and loyal to his masters.

But then man grew complacent, and greedy, and ignoble, and one by one the gods abandoned him. And as they left, the lights went out on earth, leaving man in deep confusion and despair. Eventually, only one goddess was left: Astraea, the goddess of justice. She promised to stay with mankind unless he grew so wicked that she could no longer bear the sight of him; but in the way of things this too came to pass, and so the last goddess left us. She plunged us into darkness, and took our justice to the stars. And mankind was alone and lost.

The story made Set feel melancholy. Are we still alone? he asked. Will Astraea ever come back?

Cedric grinned at his solemn brother. *Iam redit et virgo, redeunt Saturnia Regna,* he said. Virgil wrote that, boy. *With the Virgin, the Days of Old will return, too.* Perhaps when man is worthy, she will be the first to return.

Set knew Cedric meant to be comforting. But somehow, he didn't like the idea of the gods sweeping back in to take things over. That frightened him more than the idea of being alone.

He went to Oliver with his fears, and Oliver promised to cure him of gods. He collected Set and Desmond and loaded them onto the train to the city, and they walked the long blocks to a brightly colored building with gold crown moldings and loud, gaudy posters advertising something brand-new: a moving picture, Oliver called it. In large lights on the awning, a word Set tried to read, but didn't know. Nickelodeon, said Desmond, and the big man grinned like a boy. Desmond loved new inventions, new toys and technological marvels. His fascination with newness was the perfect counterpoint to Oliver's love of the old.

Oliver handed fifteen cents to the man in the booth, and they went inside. It was bare as a board, with hard seats and ugly white walls, but as soon as the picture started Set was lost onscreen. Satan gamboled and danced, the people onscreen ran herky-jerky away, fires burned and dissolved, dragons and demons sprang from nowhere and disappeared, and fantastic-looking people in paint and marvelous costumes filled the screen. And at the end, Set stood and applauded like he'd been taught, and waited for all the people and dragons to come take their bow.

It's only light, said Oliver, smiling. A projection. You don't have to applaud.

The spells the screen cast were the most marvelous sort of magic, flicker and shadow and sleight-of-hand on a grand scale. Watching these illusions play out, Set saw a world more fluid than his own, an enchanted otherworld. He often wondered after how he might slip inside it.

❖

Photograph: A fine soft layer of dust over a scattered still life. A vanity table, topped with silver-backed hairbrush, golden hair pads, glass jars filled with perfume, powder, and paints. A lady's tools of beauty, undisturbed since the night she died.

❖

Inge's father didn't mind if she played in the disintegrating parts of the manor. She sometimes slept in the old servants' quarters, watching the moon and stars through the hole in the roof. She clambered about on the old banisters and the back staircase, jumping aside hastily as bits of them crumbled. She pretended she was the pirate captain of a great but broken ship, fighting mightily to keep it from sinking, the baby willow warblers in the rafters her stalwart crew.

But she knew better than to enter her mother's bedroom. It was kept locked, and the only person with a key was her father. Once, just once, she'd found the door ajar and looked inside. Her father lay facedown across a cream lace bedspread, filthy with dust and age. He held his head in his hands and his broad back shook, and Inge found him somehow more terrifying this way than when he was yelling or glowering at her. She tried to creep back out, but he heard her and ran after, shouting all the while that he would flay the curiosity out of her hide. Cook took pity and hid her in the pantry cupboard. She could hear her father banging about, saying rude things to Cook, and he even kicked the cupboard next to her, hard enough to splinter the wood. Then he went away, his loud footsteps sounding flat and angry in the corridor. When Cook finally let her out, Inge was shaking so hard it took ten full minutes for her to stop. At dinner that evening, her father simply turned to her and held out his fork threateningly. Never, never, *ever* again, he said, and jabbed the fork into his duck so ferociously that Inge half-expected to hear it quack.

❧

Curiosity #315: Jar of children's teeth, prehistoric, date of origin unknown. Partially burned.

❧

Once, when Set was the age where fiction and reality are easily confused, Pru told him about a new book she was working on. In it, Mr. Rabbit finds a secret passageway in his little rabbit house under the earth, and the secret passageway leads to a secret door, and the secret door leads to a secret room where a secret feast is spread over a secret table.

Set was sure his huge house must have a secret room somewhere. He spent hours knocking on the walls to see if they were hollow, trying to peer behind bookcases, pressing every knot in the fireplace to see if something would happen. He had wriggled behind one of the bookcases in the library when he heard footsteps, and he stilled and silenced himself. He wasn't sure if what he was doing was punishable or not, but he didn't care to find out; Pru was a firm believer in corporal punishment and he still feared the switch.

Set heard two sets of footsteps, one light, one heavy, and then Oliver and Cedric talking—no, arguing.

We should tell him, said Cedric. When he's old enough to understand.

Tell him what? asked Oliver. That he was dead and now he isn't? What can it matter to him?

It's not right, said Cedric. And it's my fault. You can't come back from death, not really.

Set did, said Oliver, and he sounded as angry as Set had ever heard him.

Cedric seemed oddly cheerful. Suit yourself, he said. But it's cruel, if you ask me, not to let him know. Not to tell him what he is.

And what is he? shouted Oliver. Set flinched as something made a loud smashing noise. One of the busts on the bookshelves? A vase?

Don't get sore at me, said Cedric. I'm just trying to be honest, stop hiding what's plain.

Set had no idea what they meant, but it gave him shivers and made his toes curl. It made his hollow place feel wider and emptier than ever. His knees were beginning to ache from being pressed up again the bookcase, and the dust back here was in his nose and mouth and eyes, and he hoped they would leave, soon, before he sneezed or coughed.

So am I, said Oliver, forcefully. He seemed to be walking away from the bookcase, and then the footsteps stopped. It doesn't help for him to know, when he can't do anything about it.

But maybe we *should* do something about it, said Cedric. I just thought—and then footsteps, heavy and light, heading out the door and down the hall together. Set sighed and slid out from behind the bookcase, his knees pulsing with pain and pressure. He saw the little plaster bust of King George IV that usually sat on the fireplace mantel. It was shattered in a hundred jagged pieces all over the hearth rug.

Just to be quarrelsome, Inge often asked the governess, Why do we not learn Irish?

The governess always shuddered. Because it is a heathen, filthy Roman Catholic language, she would say.

But Father is Catholic, said Inge. After Inge was born and her mother died, her father had converted to Catholicism, though no one else had. Hannah said it was because their mother had been a Catholic, and their father wanted to make sure he found her in heaven. The mustachioed governess said it was because their father was under the influence of the demon lord himself, though she said it in a whisper and never when Father was around.

Albert said it was because Father was sad and lonely, and people who are sad and lonely seek comfort in strange places. Inge didn't know much about religion—though she said her prayers each night like she was taught and went to church on Sundays with Cook—but she didn't see what could be comforting about it. If she had a religion, she supposed it would be the Having of Adventures. It would involve trials of wisdom and courage, with long quests for magical objects, and one would worship in far-off lands, where natives heaved spears at one another and prayed to strange gods in fiery temples. Inge's village church was the last place in the world she'd think to Have Adventures. The church was damp and gray, and the Book of Common Prayer was boring, and the vicar was a hundred years old and asthmatic, forever coughing and wheezing his way through endless, wandering sermons. Inge sometimes wondered, sleepily, what would happen if he just dropped dead during the Eucharist. Was another ancient vicar stowed in the closet with the vestments, just in case?

But Inge's father did a lot of things that the governess was at a loss to explain, and converting to Catholicism was just one of them. The governess could not explain why he would not let the farms to new tenants, or why he let the land lie fallow and wasted. Nor could she say why he sometimes went to Belfast, and why he always came back sorrow-eyed. She did not know why he voted against Home Rule but had an angry admiration for the Nationalists, for their blasted courage and convictions, he said. The only thing she could say—indeed took great pleasure in the saying of it—was why Inge's father had not smiled nor laughed nor touched his youngest daughter since the night her mother died.

❖

The jumble of Oliver's cabinet held a few genuine treasures. The shelves were lined with gold doubloons, books plated with silver, crowns set with rubies and sapphires and emeralds. Directly under the figure of the snake, at the tail end of the cabinet, perched a meticulous jade miniature of ancient Chang An. And plenty of other goods fit for a lord lay buried under the most mundane items—a stuffed lizard with a necklace made of pearl, a medieval manuscript serving as a hiding place for a small, famous lost diamond.

But as Set grew older, his favorite object of fixation shifted from the bright shiny coins and jewels and became, instead, an egg. A fossilized egg from the moa bird, a creature extinct since the fifteenth century. Large, cream-colored, and solid as rock, it fascinated Set: a manifestation of endless possibility. He didn't know what a moa was, but he pictured all sorts of creatures—a small dragon, perhaps, or a brightly colored bird, large as the flying dinosaurs. He was obsessed with the idea that a life could be caught out of time forever, spared the fate of the rest of its kind. He would sit before it on the footstool, and sketch the egg, the thatched nest underneath, and make lists of the creatures it might contain.

Oliver found him at it one afternoon, and unlocked the Cabinet for him. He lifted the egg, put it into Set's outstretched hands. Humans overhunted them, he told Set. They looked like emus, or kiwi. Do you know what those are? Set shook his head, no. I'll show you, said Oliver, and he went off to the library, left Set holding the egg. Set was certain he felt it moving about. It made him nervous. He was sure he would drop it and a dragon would fly out.

Oliver came back with an important-looking book bound in red leather. He thumbed through until he found a faded illustration of a strange bird. Thick-legged, gray-brown, long-necked, incapable of flight—thoroughly disappointing, as far as Set was concerned. He handed the egg back to Oliver, no longer interested in its lost potential. Oliver laughed. You're unhappy, he said. I've ruined your object for you.

Set nodded, close to tears. What was the point of dreaming up new dragons now?

Oliver smiled, and knelt beside Set. You know, it's taken me many years to collect all of these things. It is a part of me now, the best part, perhaps. Oliver's beard quivered, and Set remembered being very little and watching that little triangle dance upon his brother's chin like a sail in the wind. Just like all of his siblings, Oliver seemed changeless.

Why did you? asked Set. It was the right question. Oliver's beard dipped and he showed a rare, shy smile to his small brother.

Because of the mystery, said Oliver. I find an object—it's a blank, or nearly one. And then—and then I have the pleasure, the *exquisite* pleasure, of finding the object out. What it is, where it's from, when it's from, what it does, or says, or was. Who might have loved it, and lost it, you see? What it meant to someone or something, long or near ago.

Am I a mystery? asked Set. Do I belong with the spirits?

Oliver shifted in surprise, then smiled. He kissed the top of Set's head. This is your world, too, he told Set. You belong here. Set was not so sure about that. He loved the cabinet, but he also loved motorcars and moving pictures and the momentum of modern life. Why don't you go to museums, like Cedric? he asked. Why keep these things here?

Oliver laughed. This is more than a museum, he said. These cabinets are live things, can't you feel it? These aren't Ced's dead relics, dug up and put on display for the learned. These are the things that matter to me; this is the strange wide world, right here, and he gestured at the long wall of cabinets. Well, the unfinished world, anyway. As much of it as I could fit into Mother's parlor without her scolding, he said, and unfolded himself from the floor in an elegant gesture.

Set had made a list once, of all the things he knew about Oliver. He rolled it up like a parchment and tied a blue silk ribbon around it and gave it to Desmond for his birthday. To Set's surprise, the big man began to weep when he read it, fat tears landing on the page and smearing the careful ink.

It's the best present anyone has ever given me, Desmond told him. Desmond put Set on his lap while he and Oliver sang the happy birthday song, and Oliver gave Desmond a silver pocket watch, and Desmond kissed Oliver and ruffled his pretty black hair. You're so good to me, he said. What a damned waste.

Why a waste? asked Set later, alone with Pru. Why doesn't Oliver marry Desmond?

Pru's face went as red as Desmond's, and she shook her head. You don't understand anything at all, she said.

Things About Oliver
    Mustache that dances
    White teeth
    Quite small
    Curiosity cabinet is for mysteries
    Calls Pru "Mother"
    Has a pony
    The pony is named Maria
    Loves Desmond
    Loves paintings of battles
    And ladies singing loud

❧

On the nights the wind howled fiercest through the manor, making the windowpanes shudder and the spiders scurry back into the wainscoting, Inge left her drafty bedroom to wander the wild grounds. On these nights, everything seemed to quicken and jump, jittery and glimmering in the savage moonlight. These were heathen nights, full of half-magic. On these nights, Inge was on the lookout for a faerie circle or a forgotten spell, or perhaps a doorway to someplace else entirely.

One of these nights, when she must have been about ten or eleven—old enough to be brave, young enough to be foolish— Inge had climbed out onto the roof to watch the stars light the shivering grass. She saw, so close it was like a small fire, a star plummet to earth just outside the village. She held her breath until it was down, then raced to find it.

She scoured the ground for any fading light until—yes, *there*, just outside the old blacksmith's barn, a small flickering lump in the overgrown grass. The damp was already killing it. She put a scratch down the paint on the side of the barn to mark the spot, then ran to the house to find a jar. But by the time she was back, the little star's light had gone out for good.

❧

Curiosity #798: Ballet shoes, circa mid-eighteenth century. Worn by Marie Camargo of the Paris Opera Ballet; first non-heeled ballet shoes in the history of the dance.

❧

Of all the women his elusive father maintained boisterous and public affairs with, Set liked the principal ballerina of the Ballets Russes the best. His father took him to see her dance in *Prince Igor*, elbowing Set each time her skirt flared high over her shiny pink thighs. She was very kind to Set afterward, tousling his hair and smiling a dimpled smile for him. She smelled like melted sugar and rose petals. And she gave him gifts: candies from Paris and furs from Moscow, little wooden dolls from the Ukraine that nestled inside one another like a puzzle. He sat in the corner of her dressing room and released the dolls, one by one, while his father whispered something to the ballerina that made her laugh. Set was in awe of this ability that adults seemed to possess—the creation of mirth in another human being. His father wasn't good for much else, as Pru wryly observed from time to time, but at this, he excelled. He could pull a coin from behind a child's ear, or tell jokes that even Cedric fell about laughing over, or make a pretty ballerina shake with helpless giggles. In the carriage on the way home, his father turned to Set and asked him what he thought of the dancer.

She seems like a very generous lady, said Set, after careful consideration. His father liked this response.

She is, he said. She is full of generosity. And—Set thought he winked, but it may have just been sunlight hitting his father's monocle—she's soft in just the right spots.

It wasn't until Set was almost a young man that he realized she was his mother.

Or rather, his almost-mother, as he came to think of her. After all, Cedric said, it was hardly genetics alone that made one a parent, and in Set's case (and Cedric's, and Constance's, and Oliver's) genetics had failed rather spectacularly or at least had been a one-sided affair at best. It was widely understood (but never spoken of) that Pru was uninterested in the business of *having* children, though she was very much interested in the business of *raising* them. She was a children's book author, and as such she had very firm ideas about the way to bring up useful adults. Her books were the sort of moral tales disguised as anthropomorphic animal stories that were so fashionable then, and whenever one of her children behaved badly they were forced to learn the appropriate tale by heart. Osmosis through story. Pru had similar ideas about genetic inheritance; she had hoped her children would be artists, musicians, dancers—but none of them showed the slightest leaning toward their birth mothers' talents.

Set was the last hope—Pru paid for dance lessons as soon as he could walk—but he was bored by dance and Pru's plans for him were dashed. Like everything else, she took this setback in stride. She summoned her eldest, Cedric, and arranged for Set to go with him on his next expedition to the Canadian Arctic. Set, said Pru, was finally old enough at twelve to travel with Cedric. You'll have a real adventure, she said. You'll get a chance to see the heathen up close. Set was disappointed. He wasn't sure what heathens were, but he supposed they must all be children, very careless indeed with their souls—since the sour-faced ladies at the church were always trying to save them.

Cedric was much older than Set, and in those heady days of Antarctic exploration—the age of men like Amundsen and Shackleton—Cedric, too, had distinguished himself. He'd been in high demand for his survey work, and led several expeditions to map the Antarctic coastline between Cape Adare and Mount Gauss. Before the family moved to Long Island, he'd dined with the great men of science at 1 Savile Row, had given lectures in London for the Royal Geographical Society.

But that was before the world was laid bare, the last dust blown loose from the darkest corners. Now there were no strange places, only strange peoples, and the demands of the public for their secrets. The public couldn't get enough of the exoticism of the east, the hot wilds of the south, the strange remoteness of the north. Cedric, who'd lived among the native people and depended on them for guides, for trade, and often for protection, did not like the way the so-called primitives were often portrayed in newsreels and print. He wanted to introduce Westerners to the complex societies and customs of these peoples, to show them in what he called a "humanistic light." He became fixated on this notion. And so he took a three-week film course, bought a camera, and began making documentary films about these far-flung inhabitants of the earth. Set could hardly believe it; to Cedric, mechanical marvels like film were anathema. Ced had scorned Oliver's dreamy love for this new art form. Oliver, he said, only wants to surround himself with shiny objects, like some kind of magpie. But now Cedric saw it as a way back to the past. He told Set this wasn't about the new or novel: this, he said, was about preserving the oldest ways of living.

This was Cedric's fifth trip north, to the Canadian Arctic. A certain segment of the public was wild for his films about the Innu people there. And the big fur company, Northland Trading, was happy to bankroll his efforts. But there was another reason he spent so much time with the Innu: he was trying to pin their legends down to history, to track down the ruins of a great northern city, lost and hidden. Of late, he was fixated on it. He spoke to Set constantly about it, his chance at a real discovery.

There couldn't possibly be a city here, Set said. Who would have built it?

Cedric shook his head. No one knows. The elders of the tribe speak of a place somewhere on the north coast. They say the people who built it abandoned it long ago.

The coast was a barren tundra. No trees, no rocks, just frozen ground and sea. What would they build it *with*?

Cedric smiled. Earth and whalebone, he said. The natives say these people built an entire city in the frozen ground, and stretched hides over the bones of whales for roofs. You see why it will be bloody difficult to find—an ancient city, buried in the cold earth.

Set was not sure how he felt about the Arctic. He had longed to see something of the world, to seek out a place in it, but here he felt entirely removed. He was always cold and they were always on the move and the dogs smelled bad and the humans worse and the food was dreadful and unchanging. His brother was traveling with a small film crew and a few very rough men from the fur company. Once they were in the Innu village in Labrador, the fur men settled down to hard drinking, and complained about the slow pace of Cedric's work. They refused to help with the camera or the lighting equipment, so Cedric instead trained the natives as his assistants.

Set liked the natives much better than the fur men—they taught him how to kill and skin a seal and how to start a fire and how to build an igloo properly. They seemed strong and self-reliant and not at all in need of saving, despite what the church ladies at home said. His friend Agloolik, a boy about his age, taught him how to fish through the ice. They sat companion-ably around the ice hole, as Set fidgeted and Agloolik laughed at his impatience. Agloolik asked Set what his name meant, and Set shrugged: nothing, he supposed. The Innu looked disappointed; *his* name, he said, was that of a spirit who lived under the ice. The spirit helped men to fish and hunt, and—he slapped Set on the back—so wasn't it right he was helping his friend to catch fish? Set pointed out that they didn't seem to be catching much of anything. Agloolik put a little fish down the front of Set's parka and rolled around, shrieking with laughter, as Set jumped and scrabbled and shouted that he would be tickled to death.

But then Agloolik became serious and sad. My people, he said, they say you do not have a soul the same as other men. Set was uneasy. He remembered, but did not mention, the words of the Japanese lady long ago, the argument between Cedric and Oliver he'd overheard.

Well then, he said, how do I get a soul?

I do not know, said Agloolik. But you will need one when you die, to lead you back to your body.

The fur men offered Set whisky and roared when he choked on the burn it left behind—though he did enjoy the way it warmed him from the inside, like a little candle. Pru was dead set against drink, and she always warned of its destructive powers. After that first sip, Set waited all night with dread for the signs of destruction to begin. He wasn't sure if his toes would drop off, or his face burst into pustules, or his insides collapse like a tent in the wind. He wondered how he would find his way back without his soul.

Cedric caught him staring into the fire and shook him roughly. Listen, you can't go trance-eyed out here, or you die.

But aren't I already dead? Am I my own ghost? asked Set.

Cedric's eyes narrowed, and he did not answer the question. Take off your gloves, he said, and put your hands over the fire like this. This cold, why, this is nothing. Not like sailing through solid ice. Did I ever tell you, he said, about how I filmed the pack ice on the *Intrepid*?

Set shook his head, even though Cedric had told the story many times. He liked to hear Cedric tell it.

We made a little wooden seat, said Cedric, and we tied it below the jib boom. And there I hung, furiously filming the ship as we rammed that ice. We'd ram it once, just enough to put a wedge in it, to weaken it. Then we'd fire engines and drive full speed into that wedge. We'd break that ice apart with a great, groaning crash, boy, and me hanging on for dear life with that rope around my waist, cranking my camera like anything.

◆

While Albert was away at war, Inge's eldest German cousin ran to Switzerland to avoid the fighting. Her father started calling him Fritz, though his name was Josef. Why do you call him that? she asked her father, too old to fight himself but happy to heap abuse upon the Hun at the intolerable meals he shared with her.

He's a coward, her father said, and speared his sausage.

Yes, but why Fritz? Inge kept her opinion to herself, but she did not think he was a coward. She had seen boys, her brother's age and younger, waving their hats at the women as they left, as though they were off to a great grand party. She felt a chill whenever the train left the station piled with all those young bodies. They said the war would be short, that Fritz would quickly be defeated. And why did they call the Germans Fritz, all of them, a whole nation of men and boys like the ones here in Ireland? Why did they call her cousin Fritz, when he wasn't even fighting? Wasn't her family glad of that—that he, at least, was not their enemy, that their cousin would not be the one to put a bullet in some poor Irish head? Did the Germans have names for the Irish, too? Were they mean, hard names, like the kind the Irish gave each other? And why did some of the Irish say we shouldn't be fighting in this war at all?

Her father waved away her questions with his sausage. Some

cowards might not want to fight, he said. I'd hang them right now if I could. Their place, those traitors, is on the battlefield. Just like Albert. You're a smart girl, God knows. You should understand.

But Inge didn't understand. How she could be asked to suddenly hate her cousins? Why was her father opposed to independence for Ireland? Why did the village children throw rocks at her family? Why did the butcher's son and his friends attack the village priest and tear the collar from his neck? She knew there were two wars, one in Ireland and one out in the vague wide world, but she didn't understand either one. She only knew they were taking away the only good things in her little life.

❖

Curiosity #1209: 24-inch tail feather, taken from peacock, circa 1884. Layered shades of gold, black, cobalt, navy, turquoise, viridian, teal. Brushed with the soft iridescence characteristic of the species.

❖

After Constance moved out, he heard Oliver refer to her as a "kept woman," which seemed to mean that she lived in a tidy brownstone in the fashionable part of the city, dressed in expensive furs and jewels, and was never out of bed before noon. When Pru finally allowed him to visit Constance, she summoned him in her booming, imperious way to her bedroom, where he found a gentleman wrestling with his pants and a long, languorous Constance, eating chocolates from a gold box and clad in a frothy cream peignoir. Set was mildly horrified to see she was wearing nothing underneath. The gentleman without pants appeared to be equally horrified, but Constance smiled and held out the chocolates to Set. Have one, dear, she said, and her gown fell open on a vast expanse of white thigh. Set fled in terror.

When Set was thirteen, Constance took him into the city to see a daring new showcase of very modern art. It's upsetting all sorts of dignified people, said Constance, and Set could tell she heartily approved.

The show was in a big armory on Lexington Avenue, and Set was fascinated by the strange, distorted figures. None of them were anything like the realistic paintings Pru had hanging on the walls of their home, food on tables and hunting parties and dour people looking down their noses. These were full of loud, impertinent color, of bold strokes, of strange shapes and impossible people. And the sculptures! They seemed to belong to another world entirely—so alien and unfamiliar they were.

Matisse, shouted Constance, gesturing at a naked lady tinted blue, lounging in front of a fringe of palm fronds. The fashionable people next to them glared. Constance ignored them and dragged Set over to another painting, a woman's face, cut into sharp shapes and put back together all wrong. It gave him a muddled feeling to look at it, like looking at time coming and going.

Picasso, said Constance. She smiled. Gertrude takes all the credit for him here, but I put in a good word with a certain gentleman as well. She can't claim all his successes though lord knows she bloody well tries. Set nodded, hypnotized with horror over the scene she was making. Look, *look* at that damned painting, she boomed, and tell me he isn't a genius. Her voice echoed through the hall and seemed to charm the paintings, colors leaping from their walls to be with her. Even these bold artworks couldn't fill a room like Constance. People smiled despite themselves. Set shrank down to make more room for her, just as he did with them all. Constance made both the most and least sense to Set. She reminded him of his father, of what little he remembered—the laugh, the self-assurance, the great height and massive straight white teeth. She didn't give a fig for anyone's opinion, her family's included, and Set knew that made Pru furious. She said so often. Constance seemed the most, of all his family, to belong to the outside world. Our family, she told him, their superstitions—it's all bosh. They wanted me to be a dancer, and well—look how happy I've made myself on my own damn ambitions.

No one ever quite said so, but Set at some point realized they shared a mother—for Constance was the spitting image of the pretty ballerina, though she was strong where the ballerina was soft, strident where their mother was graceful. But Constance inherited the same sweet smile and the same coaxing way with men. She told Set with pride that there were surefire ways for people to get what they wanted on this earth, and she was one of the few selfish enough to use those means—to use any means at all. It's a good life if you own it, she told him. Be your own man.

But when he returned home, there was Oliver in the parlor, making careful notes about some new artifact from the Dark Ages. And there was Cedric in the court, playing tennis with Pru in his whites from thirty years ago. And Set knew then, as he had since he'd returned from the Arctic, that whatever was wrong with him, his missing piece, his hollow—it anchored him at home as surely as if he'd never left at all. If he was going to find his body anywhere in the afterlife, he supposed he would find it here. He felt the family's pull as though caught between powerful magnets—suspended, spinning between, a little polestar.

◆

Photograph: Inge Agnew, circa 1916. Hair a pale cloud, pinned down here and there but escaping to blur the edges. Wide, high cheekbones. Lips pale, skin pale, close-up face obscuring any background.

◆

Their cook had a son who lived in the village. He came to the manor sometimes to see his mother, when the little village school was dismissed (and *how* Inge wished she were one of those students, streaming out of the one-room schoolhouse with tidy notebooks and freed-prisoner faces). And that meant seeing Inge, too—Inge who eagerly drilled him on all the town gossip and who had kissed whom and what had they learned in school. Sometimes he had good stories and sometimes he furrowed his brow and told her, in his funny accent, that he was worried about Inge and his mother. See, your father's gone papish, he'd say, and Inge didn't even know what that meant, but worried, too, in a nameless sort of way—was this the cause of the glares she got on the rare occasions when she rode her bicycle into the village? She knew the tenants had slowly moved off the land when she was small, and that her father fought with and evicted the rest. She remembered some of the ugly scenes. She knew, also, that the people in the village spoke differently, dressed differently. Inge wore her sisters' old dresses, chiffon and lace. Though they were out of fashion and moth-eaten, they were still nicer than the drab woolen frocks the village women wore. But she couldn't imagine these differences were dangerous.

Since the cook's boy was her only friend, it stood to reason his would be the first body she knew. In the moldy smell of hay

and the damp cold of the barn, she kissed him with reckless abandon, asked him to push into her like the footman used to do to
the housemaids back when they had a footman and housemaids.
I'll marry you, he said after, his young freckled face between her
breasts. She was sixteen but already bursting into something
older; soft, warm fat over coltish limbs and long muscles.

She laughed. Don't be silly, she said. I'll never marry. Why
should I?

His face darkened to red, streaked with white, and he started
to get up. She pulled him back, hands on his shoulders, and this
time her want was a little red star, was a fire in her belly, and he
couldn't help but be flamed. She felt something lovely and then,
the star, it burst, and she smiled like a Valkyrie as he said, nervous
and coltish now, *I have to go*, turned tail, and she breathed and
breathed in the barn-stained air on that flattened patch of hay.
And she learned that sex was a weapon she could wield, even and
especially as a woman. It seemed a useful thing to know.

❖

The last Arctic film proved, finally, a commercial and critical success for Cedric. He was hailed an innovative new storyteller, the
best working in this new nonfiction film medium. With close-
ups, panoramic shots, reverse angles, and tilts—he immersed the
viewer in a wholly new way. He planned to follow up his success
with a new film shot in Alaska—but the War made that impossible and curtailed, rather painfully, his wanderlust. He took a
job in Hollywood as a studio director—one he made very clear
was a *temporary position*—with Polytone Pictures. Polytone was
second-rate, but still impressively large, with two stages and an
underwater tank for filming.

173

Cedric was tasked with directing a picture about two friends who become obsessed with—what else—Arctic exploration. It was supposed to be a comedy. Set received frequent, dyspeptic letters from Cedric that winter.

My god, he wrote, the things that pass for humor with these *dreadful* picture people.

You wouldn't believe, he wrote, the depths I've sunken to.

My dear boy, he wrote, I have become the Mack Sennett of remote places. I may as well put my native ladies in bathing costumes and hire a ragtime band.

When Cedric came home for a visit, Set asked if there might be a place for him at the studio. I'll do anything, Ced, he said. I need to get off the Island. Off this coast.

You don't want to come to Los Angeles, said Cedric darkly. These people are infernally stupid. They think the Eskimo people eat something called Eskimo pie.

I don't think people actually believe that, Set said, laughing. I think they just want to be part of a fashion.

Who needs fashion? Those natives have lived that way for hundreds of years.

Except for the guns, Set said. And the clothes. And the phonograph, and—

White men gave them those things, said Cedric, cutting him off curtly. It's not part of their culture, no more than Eskimo pies.

You want them to go back to how things were? asked Set. He wasn't asking in jest—he mostly believed in Cedric's backward vision. He'd been trained up to it.

But of course it was a silly question, anyway. Cedric wanted everything to go back. He wanted his savages noble and his civilizations autocratic. He saw the modern world as a series of trivialities, increasing in insipidness, humanity an idiot scourge, etcetera, etcetera. Set had heard the endless refrain, countless times. The people were better and the world was profound. The vulgar saxophone had not yet been invented. There was art, and mystery and there were no crossword puzzles, no silk stockings, no fast women, no rouge pots, no jazz bands, and certainly, certainly there were no Eskimo pies.

You sound like an old man, Set said.

Laugh all you want, said Cedric. He preferred a world spinning slowly, a world where history was carved into heavy stone. This fleeting life, this fractured, spasmodic present—it was hardly being alive at all. One of multitudes, so much din to wade through. So little opportunity for greatness.

Pru had been certain that Cedric would rush to join up, that he would feel called to fight in some sort of outmoded patriotism. She had been absolutely sure of it. But when Set asked Cedric if he would volunteer, he spat. The War, he said, was a machine thing, an ugly new kind of fight. Chivalry won't save them, he said grimly. Valor won't save them. The whole damned world has gone mad.

❦

Once, Inge's favorite aunt came to Larne for a longish visit. Her husband had died and she wanted to be with her niece for a while, to be reminded of her eldest sister. Inge lived for her letters and now she basked in the diminutive but powerful presence of her aunt, and absorbed all the stories she could take in about her mother and her sisters and their cheerful childhood in Germany. Her favorite story was the one about the Gypsies: her aunt always began with how Inge's maternal grandmother gave birth to three daughters while living in the little village of Ludwigshafen. It sounded like a sort of fairy tale. The eldest daughter took after her father and was very pretty; the second took after her mother and was plain, but strong and good; and the third (the aunt in question) was left wanting entirely, her sick body and solemn mood bearing the hallmarks of long childhood illness: thin, weak limbs, pockmarked face, pale, wan pallor; though she was also— perhaps in some cosmic compensation—quickest and smartest. And she would marry before the second, and the second would marry before the first, and the first would not marry until her mother was dead and her father had given her up as a spinster.

One sweltering summer day the girls heard their father, who was the village *Polizeichef*, complaining about a band of Gypsies who had set up camp just outside the village. He and his friends were sitting on the porch, drinking from steins of beer in their shirtsleeves, cold rags draped over their heads.

Well, you're the *Polizei*, said Herr Baumann, the butcher. Why don't you chase them out?

It's too hot, the girls' father said. Let them keep there until it's cooler. It's too hot to go running around after a bunch of *Roma*, he said, and all the other men nodded and grunted in assent. The girls, listening through the window of the parlor, looked at one another. Gypsies! They would be dancing, singing, telling fortunes perhaps—maybe making spells! We have to go, said the eldest. Tonight, before they drive them out.

When their mother was asleep and their father had passed out in the big porch swing, the girls put on their pinafores and crept down the stairs to see the Gypsies. When they got to the Gypsy camp, they found it disappointingly small and quiet—no singing, no dancing, only a few women in brightly colored skirts cooking over a crackling fire. Four caravans, painted red and white, parked among the trees, and drying laundry was strung on lines between them. It didn't look magical, or mysterious, or particularly wicked—but for the caravans it could have been their own backyard.

The girls were about to creep away, unseen, when one of the women—a very old lady, with hair tucked under a kerchief over dark, hard eyes—put her fingers in her mouth and whistled loudly. A group of men emerged from the caravans, and one of them grabbed the eldest daughter, twisting her arm behind her back. Bring her here, said the old woman. The eldest wanted to cry out, but she was known for being brave as well as beautiful, and so she said nothing. The second, even braver than her sister, and more stubborn, too, crossed her arms over her starched white pinafore and glared at the grinning men. If you're going to eat our hearts, then get on with it, she said. We're not afraid of you.

The youngest, though, thinking quickly, pretended to cry. Let us go, she sobbed. Don't magick us, don't eat our parts, please. We only wanted to have our fortunes told.

Ah, said the old woman. You should have come in the front way like good little children. You are in luck, for here is my daughter, Nadya, who can read your life in the lines of your hand. The young woman stirring the pot over the fire nodded shyly. Come closer, child, said the old woman to the youngest, but she flinched and hid behind the second, still pretending to sob. The youngest had a certain self-preservation that would allow her, alone of all her family, to escape marriage, childbearing, and two wars unharmed.

I want to hear my fortune, said the eldest, and she shrugged free of the Gypsy's grip and held her hand out over the fire. What will happen to me?

The younger woman, Nadya, took the eldest's hand in hers and turned it over to trace the creases in the palm. She hummed to herself as she did so, some ancient, sad song, full of trouble and pain. Her face, though young, was worn, her prettiness already rubbed away in the hard road life of the *Roma*. Finally she spoke, voice still a singsong of sorts. Your heart, she said, you will find over mountains and seas, and you two will meet but late, when you've nearly lost the thread of love. She put the eldest's palm down, and smiled at her sweetly, and it wasn't until the sisters were gone, long past the caravans and out of the camp, that she turned to the old woman. She will live a short life, *bednaya devochka*, she said. Poor little girl.

The Gypsy woman was right, of course, though who can say if she foretold or forced the course of events: Inge's mother would refuse to marry and would, at thirty-three, join the German Freikorps as a nurse, following her beloved brother into the Boer War. Once there, she would watch her brother die at Elandslaagte, and nurse to health a handsome British soldier. And she would follow him back to Ireland—to her fortune, to her children, to her early grave.

When Inge's aunt got to the end, she reached for Inge's hand and told her, Never mind that last bit. I made that up, of course. To make myself feel better.

My father blames me, said Inge. He blames me for her loss.

No one, said her aunt, is responsible for the way they come into this world. But men often forget that. It doesn't do to dwell on the past, she said, and she shook her head. It's the women who usually have to remember that.

◆

Curiosity #49: Partial mermaid's skeleton, circa 1822. Discovered in the stomach of a shark caught off the coast of Iceland. Eyewitnesses gave hair color as brown, skin color as green, and sex as most likely female. The eyes, they reported, were blue as the sea.

◆

When Oliver died, Desmond stayed locked in the parlor for weeks, making furious notes in the black notebook. Then he emerged, only to vanish down the drive, Set supposed for good. Set took to hovering in the parlor's darkened doorway, watching the cold, barren fireplace as if Oliver would reappear there. He wasn't sure whether he hoped for that or not. He wasn't sure what the rules were, how you came back: how many tears shed or wishes made or memories drummed up after death.

Instead it was Desmond who came back, briefly. They sat on Pru's porch in silence. Set had heard that Desmond also had the flu, and when he came out of a three-day fever dream to find Oliver dead, he loaded a pistol and stood in front of the cabinets for a long, long time. He put the pistol in his mouth and took it out, put it in and took it out, and finally placed it on the floor and walked away.

Set had supposed Cedric never much cared for Oliver, but he seemed utterly undone by his brother's death. He took the train back from California, missing the funeral but not the opportunity to shout at them all: at Pru, at Desmond, at Constance—and especially at Set, incomprehensible madness about sacrifice and substitution. It should have been you, he told Set, and Set wept alone in his bedroom because it wasn't. Death demands a sacrifice, Cedric told Set at the dinner table, and Pru slammed down her fist so hard the pot roast jumped. She glared, and Cedric got up and left, shouting all the while in Italian, in Latin, in some other language that Set didn't know. Set stared at his potatoes, speared one with a shaking hand.

Set, Pru said. He loves you. He loves us. He's trying his best to be brave, that's all.

But Set didn't think that was all. Something happened that shook him, shattered him, and he didn't suppose it was brave, though perhaps there was a kind of love behind it. One afternoon, just before Cedric was to leave for Hollywood again, Set was in the pool, swimming slow laps and missing Oliver. He felt a hand on his neck, his head pushed down into the blue. He knew not to breathe in the water, but panicked as the hand stayed steady, kept him firmly submerged. He held his breath and tried to shake off the hand and saw the edges of his vision start to blacken and smear. Help, he thought, and the hand stopped taking life and gave it, pulled him up by his hair, dragged him off to the side of the pool and draped him there, coughing and sputtering and swearing. It was Cedric.

You were drowning, he said firmly, insistently, and his eyes were dark, his suit sopping wet.

Set stared. He clung to Cedric's suit coat, even now, couldn't pry his own hands from his older brother's arm. He gasped and flopped and coughed and clung.

You were drowning, said Cedric, but I didn't let you drown. I didn't. You should remember that.

Set leaned over and threw up his lunch in response.

He wanted to tell Pru what had happened, but he didn't quite dare. Pru was hardly herself, anyhow. She pounded the piano and tore up her latest manuscript. Her hair went white overnight. She threw her long shadow over Set after that. When she wasn't there, she asked Constance to leave her city apartment and stay with Set, who at sixteen was humiliated.

Set wanted out. His home felt like a mausoleum now. Cedric was in Hollywood making his pictures, Pru was locked in her grief, and Constance chafed at her forced return. And Oliver was clearly not coming back, in spirit form or any other. Set ambushed Pru in her bedroom, where she sat grimly pinning up her long white hair. I want to go to school, he said. Pru shook her head fiercely, scattering hairpins across the vanity. No, she said. You have good tutors, she said. It's not safe for you to leave us. We don't know what might happen. She tucked a pin expertly into the corner of her mouth and twisted a section of hair back and under.

You're all bloody mad, you know. He stopped, shrank back. He'd never spoken that way to Pru before.

Pru plucked the pin from her mouth and shoved it into the last unruly wisp. She turned to him. Insolence won't help. You'll do as you're told, and no more talk about it. And she pushed him out and shut the door. Set thought he could hear her crying softly through the oak, though he told himself he had surely imagined it.

Once the War was over, Pru had promised her own sort of familial truce. Set had high hopes, but what it amounted to was this: Pru took her youngest son to London to visit her relations, and this was even worse than the house on Long Island. Pru, her mother, and grandmother seemed to be the only people left, and the three of them in the vast house in Kensington put him in mind of Macbeth's witches. They dressed in black and spoke in whispers, and lived in a house that was nothing short of Gothic, all winding turrets and blood-colored wallpaper and old furnishings covered in sheets. They seemed to live mainly in two or three rooms, floating about the darkened house like restless spirits. His old, old great-grandmother boxed his ears with astonishing force when he put his elbows on the table at dinner. Set lay awake at night, terrified to sleep, sure they were casting uncharitable spells to fill his underwear with snails or turn his blankets to adders. Despite his misgivings, he wrote to Cedric in Los Angeles but received no reply, and became convinced the witches were burning his mail. He missed his brothers like lost limbs and the hollow inside him was growing; it hurt, he ached with it. He clung, still, was lost without them, was immensely relieved when Cedric wrote back, begrudgingly allowing him to come to California. Cedric was lonely past bearing, alone among the infidels. Perhaps, then, it was for Cedric's sake that Pru relented at last.

And so Set finally fled: he left London and the witches and the damp and the cold and traveled to sunny Hollywood, to make and sell dreams.

❖

Curiosity #680: Magicienne pre-flint lighter, automatic match variety, circa 1891. French manufacture. Steel case with intricate, abstract engravings.

❖

When the war after the War came to County Antrim, Inge's home burned. First drums, then fire, then her father put Inge and her sisters on a ship and shot himself. He sent them forth with what he had; a small but serviceable sum for passage and a few months' food and shelter. The adult sisters now split from each other at the first port of call. Hannah went west, Clara went north; and Inge took a sack of books and a compass and hitched a ride on a steamer headed south. At eighteen she had some vague idea of a warm wind and a bright smudge of horizon, and an undiscovered island littered with coconut trees. She dreamed of sleeping under the stars, of fleeing the damp chill of her homeland.

And so the Agnew sisterhood, never strong, dissolved like mist, and so the sisters were borne across vast oceans. The little figures moved over the waves, a tiny diaspora over the navy night of the seas.

Inge's full name was Ingeborg Adelaide Cecilia Agnew. The Adelaide was pure ornamentation, but the Cecilia substantive; it was after her English grandfather, Cecil. She wasn't sure how so much of a name could seep into the blood, but she had been astonished to learn about his history after she wrote to Hannah about her new life. He lost his mind while stationed in the Transvaal, and once home, ran off (wrote Hannah, disapproval dripping from her careful round script) with a bareback rider in the circus. He gave his lands and title up to his younger brother to follow her, and returned alone four years later without a word of explanation. He mostly took up where he had left off, a stranger to his furious wife and his now-nearly-grown son—Inge's father. He came back with nothing except a large black bag full of photographic equipment. He never said where it came from, and when his younger brother died, he moved the family to Larne to take over the family estate there as he'd been meant to do. But he remained passionately committed to photography for the rest of his life.

When Inge set out, she knew none of this. Her grandfather was merely a portrait in the hallway, bearded and pale and deadly dull. She supposed she would be the same someday, and that some distant relation would be astonished to find this dry ancestor capable of acts of great passion. She was all long limbs and huge eyes, and she couldn't run fast enough or see far enough to take the world in as she wanted to. So she took up photography as memory; she bought her first camera, a folding Kodak Brownie. She got it at one of her first stopovers, from a one-armed ex-whaler from Portsmouth living in Portugal with his common-law wife and children. He would bring his fish to the market and quote Shakespeare quite badly to anyone who would listen. He was Inge's first friend, and though she knew he was mixing up Edgar and Edmund, still she loved to hear him pour forth Lear's melancholy in his greasy, grizzled tones. She traded him her copy of *The Collected Sonnets* for the camera—that and a ride on his boat to the next seaport town.

❖

In Hollywood, Set loved to stand outside the studio and watch the chaos: beautiful women and men in costume, stagehands carrying backdrops and set pieces and props, cars and trucks and buggies, and especially the endless menagerie of animals: horses and bears and lions and tigers and cats and dogs and peacocks and orangutans and every kind of bird imaginable. Set even saw an octopus once, carried about in a giant glass tank by four men. It was rather small and sulky.

While Cedric was on set, Set spent long hours sitting at the commissary making sketches of the local wildlife. One of the studio executives sat next to him one day at lunch and leaned over to see his drawings. Might as well make use of you while you're hanging about, he told Set, and hired him on the spot as a captioner. Set was tasked with writing and illustrating captions for the intertitles, those floating dialogue screens. He liked best to draw birds and other things with wings. He charmed one of the stars of Cedric's stable with a pair of origami swans, and twining from their beaks like ribbon, the words "You are as lovely and wild as the swans at Coole." The actress, a vain, pretty thing, had never read Yeats but she murmured it like a mantra as he took her to bed that night. He took a fair number of women to bed. He was drawn to this new, bold kind of girl—these were brash, self-made beauties. And they were drawn to him, to his bright throwback beauty and his cool remove. Set had been shocked, almost, that he hadn't simply disappeared, dissolved like smoke, the further the train took him from his family home. But it seemed he was substantial, not quite spirit-stuff, not in body, anyway. And a fair number of women at the studio seemed concerned primarily with the body. A fair number of men, too. Adonis was the name that stuck at Polytone, half in flattery, half in farce.

Set quite liked California, in spite or perhaps because of it being so very different from New York. He liked the unsettled, seedy feeling of the place, the way the ground could actually shift under one's feet—he'd always liked literal metaphors like that. He liked how there was a strange and wonderful self-sufficiency to the small shops scattered along the highways into town—palm readers butted up against fruit sellers butted up against one-pump filling stations and two-bit diners with grass-thatched roofs, the whole thing dotted and crosshatched with garish bill-boards. The swaying palms suggested a lazy paradise, but this part of the world was full of hustle, because everyone—from the men picking apples in the Valley, to the old ladies selling chiles, to the bit players clustered and queuing up for the next walk-on—

everyone understood there was something new here, a second sort of gold rush for those willing to jump and run. Here, it was all flash. You could eat your dinner in a restaurant shaped like a hat. You could drink your Manhattan in a tiki hut. A sea of neon signs swarmed the airspace above the buildings, advertising dancing, girls, drinks, food, footwear, fashion, even faith; the religious revival shows that came to town would park in one of the big empty lots and throw up flashy signs with arrows pointing like the hand of god.

But Cedric still hated it. He complained that the people were loud and vulgar, that the heat made his bones hurt, that he felt he was falling off the edge of the world.

Set supposed it must look strange, the age difference between Cedric and himself. He was embarrassed by Cedric for the first time, and he was glad the people here didn't seem to hold his brother's behavior against him. Back home Cedric made sense. Old money was allowed its eccentricities. It was possibly expected of them.

They never spoke of the swimming pool.

❦

Photograph: Snapshot of a pile of maps, folded and refolded and brightly colored. One shows elevation, one shows rivers and lakes and tributaries, one promises adventure: strange lands unseen by human eyes.

❦

For her nineteenth birthday, Inge got herself a new camera and a commission from *National Geographic*. In Buenos Aires, she'd met a photographer from the magazine who wanted to sleep with her, and—fascinated by the idea that one could be paid for one's work—she took frank advantage. Sex in exchange for a leg up, so to speak. She began to make use of her novelty, as the rare female adventurer. It often gave her more access, more trust among the peoples she was photographing. The magazine saw her value, and kept her on. She wondered what the mustachioed governess would say, and smiled with no small pleasure at the thought.

This time, she caught passage with a group of anthropologists on their way to study a remote island, where the natives tattooed their bodies and faces with a sharp shell and a paste made of coconut ash. The scientists had traveled there to study the rigid caste society, and the way the tattoos reflected each individual's place in the group. Inge took photos of the beautiful, intricate designs; no straight lines, only curved and swirling marks, dark circles opening to spirals. Each body was a universe, marked by many galaxies.

The scientists were older, Dutchmen, and they ignored her and spent evenings smoking in their separate camp. She was much more interested in the people of the island, and they were intrigued by her. They touched her hair and asked questions and, according to the interpreter, they called her Cloud Woman. Cloud Woman, they asked her, why is your skin so blank and empty? How did you drain the color from your hair? What is a photograph? She showed them the photographs after she'd developed them, told the people they would read like dreams to others. They told her the tattoos were maps, so that after they died, their spirits would know how to find their homes in the afterlife.

Cloud Woman, the women asked, where are your children? Where is your man? When she laughed and told them she had neither, they looked at her gravely, disapproving. You must find them, they said.

Before she sailed, she let them tattoo a small black cloud on her foot. This way, they told her, you will always know yourself. Perhaps it was the fermented island drink, but that warmed her somehow. Despite the pain, she felt a strange sense of comfort in the mapping of her own skin.

◆

Set liked it here in the sun, and these picture people forgave him his own reserve, mostly because he was friendly and graceful and of course, so very pretty. He'd never known he *was* before; it made him a little selfish and a little sad, too, because the brightness covered up the dark pull down he often felt. He wondered that no one else could see it. He laughed, often, not because he was joyful but because it was easy to let your mouth fall open here. Ease was easy to fake. Hollywood attracted the strange, anyway—Set was in a sense just one more sideshow attraction, the beautiful man with a hole where his soul ought to be.

But Cedric stuck out like a relic. He seemed drawn in different, drabber paints, a strange figure against the bright Los Angeles landscape. People here lived fast, but easy—just the opposite of meticulous Cedric. He could spend years on a dig; he'd spent decades just mapping the Antarctic. He didn't understand this place, so new and full of cheerful ruthlessness. Set was hardly surprised when one day he returned to their rented bungalow and found Cedric on the porch, his bags at his feet, his frozen expression a thousand miles away.

You're going away, Set said. He'd expected it.

We're going away, boy, said Cedric. Go and get your things together. We must be at the station, in one hour sharp.

Set envisioned sitting on the train in defeat, winding through the San Gabriel Mountains, watching the bustle recede and fade into landscape. Why? he asked.

Cedric grinned. My city, he said. My city has been discovered at last!

I don't know what you mean, said Set.

The lost Arctic city, said Cedric. The one the Innu spoke of.

I thought that was a myth, Set said. Just a story.

Myth is often something more, said Cedric, and he laughed. Whale bones, boy! The coastal natives found an entire pitful, at Point Hope. Point Hope! It begs the impossible, does it not? I received the telegram just this morning.

Set sat down slowly on the porch swing. He rocked, and rocked, and did not look at Cedric; felt the cold disapproval rolling over him just the same. I'm not going, he finally said. There was a long, long silence.

And after, though Cedric shouted at him for a quarter of an hour, though he called him all sorts of rude and unfilial names, though he threatened and cajoled and pleaded, Set would not be moved. In the end, Cedric went to find his lost city alone, and Set stayed and took over Cedric's film. He chose to stay, in the sun, out of the shadow of Ced's obsession. For the first time in his life, he was finally free of his family. Free, or adrift. He wasn't sure which.

❧

On her twentieth birthday, Inge received word that her sister Clara had died. She did not attend the funeral. She had written to Clara, at the beginning of the sisters' separation—some small concession to the blood they shared—but Clara never replied. Inge was hardly surprised; they were like strangers to each other.

And so she wrote to Hannah instead: dull, disapproving Hannah, who could not resist writing sanctimoniously back. She enjoyed the victory of virtue. *I am in lovely, lively Rio*, Inge would write to Hannah, and Hannah would write back, *You are in the lap of mortal sin*. That sort of thing. Hannah did not approve of Inge's hand-to-mouth existence, of her vocation. It was 1920, Inge wrote her, prickly. Perfectly acceptable for women to have careers of their own. Father's money had long since run out, and how else was she expected to eat? She could marry, wrote Hannah, and Inge laughed to think of such a thing. Who on earth would she marry? And why, when she could travel alone with all the freedom she liked? When she could document the wilds of the world?

So instead of dutifully heading to Finland, where Clara had died in childbirth like their mother, or slinking off to Hannah in Newfoundland, sins unrolled before her—Inge made her first dirigible flight. She'd read about this miracle, this new weightless ship in the sky, and though there were no commercial flights yet, she managed to make herself very charming to a military pilot taking a test run, from Rio de Janeiro to Friedrichshafen. She shared his cabin, and she was happy to be a *Hure* for the chance to fly, to skip from shore to shore like a gull. Once on land, she decided to find her mother's people, but when she wrote Hannah from Germany, her sister wrote back that she had no idea how to find them. Her beloved aunt had left Berlin after the War with no forwarding address, just disappeared, and the relatives in Ludwigshafen were all dead or dispersed. Hannah wrote that it was just the two of them now, but it might as well be that she had no sister at all, so slight was Inge's sense of filial duty.

Inge sat at a café on the Bodensee and read the letter three, four, ten times. The other patrons cast suspicious looks her way—there was a deep distrust of foreigners in Germany after the War, and though she looked the part, her German was poor and marked her out.

When they were children, Hannah sometimes brushed Inge's hair until her younger sister's scalp bled. She'd scowl, as if it were Inge's fault that she was born with her hair in knots. But then there was this, also. When Inge was six, she dreamt her father had become a vulture, was waiting for and willing her death. His red eyes reeked of ugly, carrion thoughts. She woke, crying, and crept down the hall to Hannah and Clara's room. Clara put the covers over her head, but Hannah invited her in. You may stay with me tonight, she said, and tucked her arm around the young Inge as though she were a well-loved doll. And Inge was warm, and—so briefly!—happy.

We are, thought Inge, such a strange series of beings. No constancy among us. Tomorrow she would develop her zeppelin pictures—surely *National Geographic* or *Travel* would snap them up—and try to scrape together passage for the first ship she could find. But now, she sat and watched the wind roll over the Bodensee, rippling the waters and moving restlessly on.

◆

Curiosity #84: Aztec volcanic rock sculpture, circa fifteenth century A.D., probably made for the temple of Tenochtitlan. An example of a traditional demon princess, or Cihuateteo, who escorts the sun from the underworld each morning, she wears a simple skirt, breasts bared, hair long and over her shoulders.

◆

The truth about Set is the truth about all ghosts: there is a weightlessness that keeps them fluttering, light as leaves—and in turn they are drawn down to instability, to the volatile, to cracks that open and can split whole mountains. To the volcanoes. Specifically, in Set's case, to Lana Volcana.

That wasn't her real name, of course, or even her screen name. But it was what they all called her after her breakout picture, *Vera and the Volcano*—a two-reeler about an island girl that sent her star up and up. LANA VOLCANA! the picture magazines screeched, with accompanying photographs of a dark-haired vamp in a grass skirt and clamshell top. The IT GIRL, the papers called her, a new kind of girl for these daring times. *Filmstar Rag* said she was the girl you don't bring home to mama.

In Hollywood, Set found that alone among the beautiful people, his hollow place itched, emptier than ever. He had love affairs, of course, but he could find no way to feel love for the pretty young women he admired. Up close he found people attractive but flawed; there was an eagerness for closeness that repelled even as it attracted him. He worried that perhaps he could not love, and so he chose the fire that burned the brightest and he jumped in headfirst. Worry about scars later, he told himself. He needed to see if he could ever be warmed, if others could be warmed by him. Never mind his own emotions; was it possible to love a dead man?

Lana and Set first collided when Set was desperately searching for a leopard for a reshoot of a scene from his latest nature documentary, *In the Jungle*. Lana kept a pet leopard, Leopold, and she brought him in and ensnared Set in the first five minutes. Set had never seen a woman with a leopard on a leash, though he'd heard the stories. He'd heard, and soon discovered it was true, that her chauffeur drove her about in a black Rolls with white velvet interiors while her two Russian wolfhounds hung their heads out the windows in a most undignified fashion. Set supposed she must love animals. But she loved one thing only: spectacle, and anything that helped her to make it. She was drawn to Set because he was pretty, and putty in her hands. That was all she ever needed of men. (It was whispered that her real fire was reserved for women, but it would not be until her lonely later years, doing film rag interviews for cash in her motel room, that she would admit the truth of this.)

Lana Volcana believed in self-improvement. She encouraged Set to quit the studio and set up his own production company. You need to be with the brightest stars, she would say, and he would think first not of Greta Garbo or John Barrymore, but of Cassiopeia, of Orion, of the gods and demigods of the prominent constellations. Lana herself was briefly the brightest star of them all, burning with a fierce intensity, given to passionate histrionics and an outsize sense of drama. She was famous for her fame even in a town where that was quickly becoming the rule, rather than the exception.

That winter, Lana bundled Set off to New York City and made him dance till 4 a.m. at the Stork Club's big bash. She was fried on gin when she introduced him to Carl Akley Jr., but he and Carl liked each other just the same. Carl had met Cedric years ago, and he made Set promise to come by the American Museum of Natural History, where he'd introduce him to the people who helped set up the expeditions. They needed a good director.

That year, Set surprised himself and everyone around him by moving forward, something he'd never done by himself before; he took Lana's advice and started his own company. The company lived and shot in Kenya that first year, and made four pictures for the AMNH: *African Adventures, On Safari, Big Cats!*, and *Welcome to the Wild*. Set thought back to that nickelodeon theater and wished Oliver were still living and able to see what he'd done. Sometimes he dreamed of Oliver. He dreamed a great tall tree with a multitude of branches, growing far into the heavens. He dreamed he watched Oliver climbing, climbing, small and smaller still until he disappeared altogether into the city of the gods.

When he returned, Lana begged him to take her on his next trip to Africa. I want to see the apes, she told him. Are they really like giant, hairy men?

Nothing like, Set assured her, but she purred as if he had never spoken. Set always felt he was talking to a moving picture screen instead of a live human woman. Set, Set, Set, she would scold, her voice thick with her hidden New Jersey accent and gin. Don't you ever wanna *be* somebody? Don't you ever wanna have a *passion* for something? She loved his beauty, but she despised his placid solemnity, and what was worse, his lack of interest in his own advancement. She was a fiercely smart, self-made woman. She'd escaped a typically broken home, mother on the bottle, stepfather slaphappy, sisters stupid and stuck. Dirty faces and everybody dull, dull, dull. She'd washed her own face and sewed a dress for herself from scraps she begged at the Macy's department store where her sister Maureen worked, and she'd shipped herself out at sixteen to Hollywood. The pictures were barely in their infancy, but she was smart enough to recognize a sure thing when she saw it. Sometimes, when she got too unbearable and he didn't mind the eggshells, he'd slip and call her Dottie. That was her real name: Dorothea DeRosa, though her mentor renamed her Svetlana, and her publicity people put it about that she was a Russian princess who came to Hollywood for refuge during the

Revolution. Of course, alone with Set and a few too many martinis, she slipped back into her flat native tongue and her Dottie DeRosa manners.

You have no *passion*, she'd repeat.

You're drunk, Dottie, go to sleep, Set would amiably say, and arrange her on the bed in a way that wouldn't hurt when she woke. He would never tell her, but he was disappointed by the lack of fire behind the flame. Lana was just another Hollywood hustler. And so, he supposed, was he.

We're all just illusions here, aren't we, he said, and turned her face to the side so she wouldn't choke in her sleep.

✦

Photograph: Tahitian woman, circa 1922. She is surrounded by lush foliage. She is very young, her brown face smooth, her dark eyes framed by dense black brows. Her stomach is gently rounded, her hand resting lightly over it. She does not smile.

✦

Dearest Hannah, Ma Seule Soeur,

Greetings from Paradise! I know you are unhappy with my travels and I hope, concerned with my safety. But you shouldn't be, sister. The people here are lovely and Manam is truly an earthly marvel. I wish never to leave it. I have taken wonderful photographs here and the magazine will pay me handsomely for them. The people here are much freer, much more open with their bodies, as is fitting in this climate. There is a different kind of air in this part of the world; even the stars are different to the ones we know. It is too warm to wear so many clothes, and they laugh at me in my linen blouses and long trousers. *I would laugh also. I am not one of them, and must maintain my own kind of decorum, but there are hot humid days when I long to run about in a grass skirt and brightly colored puka necklaces.*

The men have made carvings for me and tell the story of their god, the volcano. It is, they say, a quiet god, for generations silent, and they spend much time appeasing him. Last week they killed a wild boar and held a great feast, and I must say, I have never tasted anything so delicious as wild pig roasted on a spit. You should try it, should you ever get the chance, though I suppose there are not many wild pigs where you live.

I shall stay here until Christmas; then, with a sad heart, sail for Hollandia, where I will wait for my English friend and his boat. Then we travel to America. I think I will eventually set out for the West. There is a magazine out there looking for someone to cover the pictures, to capture these new exotics, the film stars, and put them on display for the public to gawp at. I'm game! I'll approach them like the wilder animals they are, these motion picture people. I'll catch them out, spots and snarling teeth, and make them something of a modern-day miracle; something truly new.

Yrs, wandering in this wide forest,

Gretel/Ingeborg

❧

Inge lands in Set's shadow long before he sees her. She knows of his reputation around the studio, a sort of junior ladies' man, and she photographs several erstwhile girlfriends of his. Her curiosity is piqued. What a cad he must be, she thinks. She's already made her mind up not to date picture people, but still she can't help but be awed by how preternaturally lovely so many of them are.

She normally spends her days off holed up in her rented room, flopped across the quilt in her slip, reading the books that she borrows from the Hollywood Library. This heat is very different from the slow, languid heat of the tropics. It's a dry heat, and it burns the throat. She waits until the iceman comes each Saturday and begs the landlady for a few slivers off the block to roll around on her tongue. Her landlady, the elderly widow of a former prospector-turned-respectable-businessman, calls her Worm, as in bookworm. The landlady's son, a car salesman, is in love with Inge. He is forever trying to sell her love along with driving lessons. She laughs and tells him she'll take the driving lessons, anyway. The landlady's son is nearly fifty, with a blanket of fat and a wide, shiny part in his sparse pale hair. His eyes shine and he sweats, *exudes*, when he sees her. He reminds her of a sea slug. She has photographed him several times, a fascinating example of the local fauna. She knows how to flatter.

She is flooring it in the salesman's brand-new 1922 American touring car, scattering birds and extras and pulling up hard to the studio gates. She leans out the window and waves to her friend, a wardrobe girl and sometime actress named Vicky. I'll be blowed, says Vicky, bringing her new beau up to stroke the car like a big bronze cat. Look at this ride!

And who's this? asks Inge, while the sea slug fumes in the passenger side. I thought you were with Adonis?

Oh, says Vicky, and makes a sour face. She's a middling pretty English girl with an exceptionally pretty bosom, and marks time mostly in the big dance numbers. Sometimes they sponge her down with dye and put her front and center in the harems. Once she even kissed Valentino. He's a cold bloke, that one. And only going after the big stars, Inge, so don't get any funny ideas. He's taken up with Lana Volcana.

Inge laughs. I don't expect that'll last long, she says. Nobody does with her.

It don't matter, says Vicky. This here's Tony. He does stunts, proper ones, falling out of windows and getting smashed with chairs and things. She beams. Tony is indeed a tower of muscle, tall and sinewy and broad-backed, with a pair of girlish brown eyes and a nice hard chin. He extends his hand and grins, and the horn in the touring car goes off, loud and abrupt and deafening. The sea slug is using it to demonstrate his displeasure.

Pleased to meet ya, says Tony. And if you're looking for Adonis—he jerks his head—he's over there. Coming out of the diner.

The salesman moves his hand to the horn again and Inge smacks it sharply. Lovely to meet you, Tony, she says. We've got to be going—ta, Vicky!

Ta, Inge, says Vicky, but Inge's already backing out of the drive with a loud squeal, and the sea slug is breathing fast. His usual milky color has deepened to a disturbing pinkish-beige. You all right, love? Inge asks.

Eyes on the *road*, the salesman tells her. And they almost are on the road, her eyes, except for the moment when they pass the diner and Inge takes in the tall young man with the beautifully louche posture. He looks sad. Not like any Casanova she's known. He glances at the car, and his fingers are long on his cigarette, and her face flushes, hands tighten on the wheel. Lana doesn't bother her. But why this one? She seems to recognize something in him, something tragic in his lonely, unguarded look. She wonders if she's making a mistake, if she might be misjudging him. Imposing her own sense of isolation.

But then, she's always been a traveler. And here, she supposes, is an intriguing trip to take. She slams on the brakes and opens the door, leaves the sea slug salesman gaping from the passenger side.

Set laughs as this strange girl rushes him, the loneliness in his face melting imperceptibly into amiable reserve. Can I buy you lunch? she asks.

I've already had it, he tells her. And I should probably also tell you: I belong to Lana Volcana. Her exclusive property and so forth. He smiles.

Inge rolls her eyes. I just wanted to buy you a corned beef sandwich, not take you to bed, she says. People in this town.

He laughs now and it's a lovely, musical sound to Inge's ear. Light and sweet, almost girlish. I'm sorry, he says, and runs his fingers through his pomaded hair. How about a coffee, then? Inge knows she's going to have to work to fall out of love with him now. She nods, and follows him back into the diner. The sea slug has since driven away, and damn, but she doesn't suppose she'll get another driving lesson now.

⬦

Set laughs because the creature flinging herself from the car reminds him, briefly, of Constance. But of course they are nothing alike except in impulsiveness, perhaps: this woman is short, all scent and hum, all soft, draped curves, and ample breasts and hips and gently rounded face. Her pale yellow hair is bobbed but escapes its style with a joyful sort of will. She is altogether unfashionable, like a girl from fifteen years ago, and he finds her deeply charming.

Now she sits across from him, dipping her toast in her tea and telling him unbelievable stories of photographing native tribal dances in the Brazilian forest. He has no idea whether he should believe her or not, though he supposes he has no reason not to. She seems smitten with him—the kind of utterly guileless person who doesn't care to hide it, though there is something else besides frank need behind her soft hands and quick words. He catches her staring, several times, in what he might call pity, were there not so much recognition in the glance. Empathy, perhaps? He notices she has not once spoken of her family, and even when she spins her tales, they're always in the present tense. He lights a cigarette and leans back, fascinated by this new creature.

And so they fall: Inge hard, like a character in a book; Set into something like a spell, a way of being at least caught if not quite in love. And so the trail of their time together grows.

Ticket stubs: Fairbanks' latest picture, *The Thief of Baghdad*. Symphony concerts. Cedric's last film, finally opening without him.

Photographs: Fooling around in the studio's studio after hours, Set in the lens, leaning into the shadow. Fuzzy and indistinct, all light and dark—no hard edges.

Souvenirs: playbills and commissary receipts and napkins filled with his sketches and her doodles and gossip about the guy on the corner stool, the starlet sipping coffee under red raw eyes.

Lists: What he should do about Lana. What she should say to Valentino if she photographs him. Their favorite songs. Their favorite pictures. Where they'd live if they could live anywhere. (Tahiti, L.A., Paris, Kenya. Long Island does not make the list.)

Eventually, Set's earliest memories. Eventually, Inge's memories of Albert. Eventually, their first memories of each other.

Doubts: his, always his. She deserves more than a ghost, more than a half-love. She has no doubts, no doubt a failing too, but possibly a more romantic one. She thinks he might be a little bit unstable, but really, who isn't?

The pull of home: he does not have the benefit of fire, the past torched clean. She is propelled, but he is compelled; he knows he can only stay so long outside the family lines. The only question is, will she come with him when it's time to go? Or maybe also: does he want her to? Or maybe, finally: would it help him to find what's missing?

❧

Set is sitting on a porch stoop on the back lot, flicking cigarette ashes at anyone who gets too close. He is the angriest Inge has ever seen him. Usually he's so implacable. Sometimes so much so that she wants to slap him just to leave a mark on that perfect face. But today that face is red, that smooth brow scrunched. I hate it, Set says. I hate being disappointed by people. I can't think of anything that's worse. His set designer has fled to Mexico with a pregnant sixteen-year-old ingenue. It's caused a smallish scandal and a giant hole in Set's production schedule. And he misses Cedric rather more dreadfully than he thought he would. He has taken very personally the thumb's-width stack of letters stamped "Return to Sender," the only break in his brother's long silence.

Inge laughs and watches the sun climb down from the sky, a glowing yolk suspended. She lifts her face to catch the last of the rays, and Set watches her with appreciation, momentarily distracted. In these last few months they've come to know each other so well, yet there is still so much mystery to sift through. They meet for dinner almost every night at the diner shaped like a hat. Lana doesn't know because she doesn't dine until at least ten. Or sometimes at all, depending on how much she's had to drink.

That's why I try to find out ahead of time, Inge says.

Find out what? Set pulls out his cigarettes, lights another, offers one to Inge. She refuses with a face. It's become a ritual already.

Find out if people are going to disappoint you, says Inge. You can tell, usually. So then you know, and you get it out of the way. Then you won't be disappointed later.

Am I the kind of person who disappoints? asks Set.

Inge closes her eyes, considers the question. I don't know, she says. With you, it's hard to say. I suppose, yes, because of what I want from you, she says, and sighs.

What do you want from me? he asks.

She smiles, grabs him by the lapels, and hauls him up and into the plywood doorway to nowhere. She is surprisingly strong.

What are you—?

Shhh, she says. Then she pulls up her skirt and puts his hand on her bare thigh, on the skin above where her stockings stop. He blinks, face locked, and she holds her breath, ready to let him have her right there in the doorway if he wants to, this beautiful, damaged boy. She wants so desperately to make him whole.

What Set likes best about Inge is how utterly human she is. In high heat she breaks out in small blisters across her back and chest, and no matter how she pins her hair it's all escaped by midday. She clears her throat when she grows bored, and loathes opera, and her front tooth is chipped from a game of blindman's bluff gone wrong when she was ten. She fidgets constantly and eats too quickly, like a starving person, and she drinks too much, and the colors she loves to wear don't suit her at all. She has a slight lisp and dances badly and calls him *dahling* only half in jest and one eye is slightly larger than the other and her toes are bulbous and she mispronounces words with great authority and she's far too fond of garlic and she laughs too loud and she doesn't know how to talk about so many things, like money. She would be, he admits, so easy to make love to, to push up against, to nuzzle and grab at and rub and tickle and cradle and with so much flesh, so much white and pink flesh to take by the armful, the legful, the bellyful.

But of course he can't do anything of the sort. Not just because of Lana. Because of his hollow place—what he knows, now, must be his inability to love. He pulls back, straightens his shirt, breathes. You know I can't, he says.

You see, she says, and sighs. Disappointing.

❖

Photograph: Close-up of a neon sign, a pair of godly hands in prayer. The sign is smeared against the night sky like a garish constellation.

❖

Inside the tent, a preacher in a spotless linen suit is singing, *Praise, praise Him, praise to the Lord.* The bleachers are crowded with people waving paper programs in front of sweating bodies and waiting to be saved. Set finds them creepy, dough-faced and blank. Inge winks at him, asks, Don't you want to be saved, my son?

I don't think I can be, he says, and he means it. She frowns and tries to smooth her frizzy hair, with the usual failure. They thought it would be funny, sneaking off to the revival. But now they're both reminded of the thing Set lacks. He's told her about the bear, about the way he's sure he died and didn't quite come all the way back. He's told her about everything, almost. He's not sure what he's doing here with Inge, why he's let her into his life. I think I died when I was small, he tells her. I think I'm stuck in two worlds now.

Like Tam Lin, she says, smiling. The Queen of the Faeries has your soul.

Who's Tam Lin? he asks.

Just a very old story, love, about a boy who belongs to two places, two women. Never mind, she says, I'll save you. How *do* I save you, anyway? She says it as a joke, but they both understand, instantly, that she will do it, will do anything he asks. He may not be dead but it's clear he's lost, and Inge is haplessly in love with him, and suddenly the revival doesn't seem so strange after all. Miracles for sale. All these people sweating through their hope, pinning the impossible on a suave old man in a cheap suit, on a plywood stage and their Sunday best and the wild dream that their lives could be different if the neon hand of god was pointing down at them.

You make everything look so easy, love, says Inge. That's a very attractive thing. Life is struggle enough—people want to admire someone who seems to be doing it better than the rest of us. Coming through it swimmingly.

Set didn't want to say so, but swimming was the wrong word; it was more floating, really. He floated along, caught in the wake of his family's vast ship. Wherever they sailed, he drifted behind, content to splash about in their eddies, then bobbing aimlessly on his own in California until Lana towed him one way and then Inge another. No wonder it looked easy. He had no soul to anchor him. He was air, was water, was as elemental as the wind. He was something much darker, too. His hollow was a great chest pain, and he suffered sometimes from world-blackening headaches. He was unable to pin down his melancholy. He half-wished he'd stayed dead after the bear. At least he would be worth something, weigh something. Bones and earth. At least he would belong to himself.

I'll save you, said Inge. I'll find a way. We'll get away from here, go to Kenya. We'll film a lion pride, live in a house by the lake there. I'll build it for you with my own two hands. Your Faerie Queen will never find you, and she kissed him, threw her ridiculous little arms around him, and he found himself kissing her back and he didn't know why but he kept on kissing her—*Praise the lord*—and she tasted like strawberries and yes, honey, manna from heaven—*Praise the lord, praise the lord of heaven above*—and Lana would set fire to his bed if she knew—*Praise and glory to the highest*—and he wondered, wildly, if maybe she actually could save him, impossible Inge. He wanted so much to let her try.

◆

Dearest Unbending Hannah,

There are no anchor points here in Hollywood. I do not understand why we try to describe this fixed place, this telescoped speck in the universe—why we try to drape this world in words, as if that could hold or encompass it. I suppose we must try because how else to say what we long for? And that is per-

haps what is hardest of all: to be full of such longing—for stone, for onions, for soap, for dawn, for familiar skies, for the dreams of others. Don't you yearn, most desperately, to know if other people's dreams resemble yours? I dream sometimes of an ash, an oak, and a hawthorn, circling a bright green patch of over-grown grass. The green is brilliant, dazzling, like emeralds, yet no sun shines—the light comes from within. What does this mean? Is it something I saw in childhood? Is it some vision sent by the daoine sídhe? *A secret mound of the faerie folk?*

Do you have such dreams, Hannah, when you close your eyes, your children down for the night? Do you dream of the land, of that strange thing they say we Irish all share? Do you dream of something like home?

I remain, forever yours in blood,

Ingeborg

◆

Curiosity #145: Stuffed albino crocodile, origin unknown. Glass eyes. Some scales missing or damaged on underside and left rear leg.

◆

The museum was short on money for its new African hall, and so they sold some of Set's films to an eager young businessman who planned to set up his own picture business, specializing in what he called "animal adventure pictures." Set had no idea until the eager young businessman called him, demanding more. I want a picture shot in Kenya, he said. Charging elephants, lions, croco-diles on the riverbank, all of that.

Tanganyika, thought Set. Paradise Lake. Where the great African explorers went looking for the source of the Nile.

He told the eager young businessman, yes. Yes.

Let's make this picture about the lions, said Inge, between bites of corned beef.

You can't go, said Set. You know that.

She frowned at him. You mean you don't want me to go.

Well—

Is Lana going? She held her breath. He had never broken it off with Lana, in part because he didn't see why he should. They were all having fun, weren't they?

Alone in her rented bedroom, Inge sometimes cried to think of all the fun they were having. She thought of leaving again, hitching a ride on a packet boat to someplace exotic. But the thought made her head ache and her heart lurch about in her chest.

After all those unanswered letters, Set knew better than to write to Cedric again, but he wished his brother could come along. He wished he could ask Cedric what to do about Inge. Set thought about calling Pru, but he didn't suppose he should bother her with his worries. Still, he *was* worried. Cedric had always included him in his adventures. And here he was keeping secrets from him. Set didn't know what to make of it. In the end, he called Constance instead, who seemed thoroughly annoyed. Leave Cedric be, she told him. Attend to your own life, your own future.

But what about his lost city? said Set.

Look, I'm not trying to be unkind, said Constance, but I'm telling you, don't make Cedric's mistakes. Go forward. There's no flying back to the far-gone past.

Set and Inge are dancing in Inge's rented bedroom, lurching into bed and table and making lopsided, monstrous shadows on the walls. They stomp out a rough waltz to the three-four time of the landlady's polka music playing below. Laughing, breathless, half-drunk, they careen around, Inge attempting to mimic Set's easy grace. She finally stumbles, sinks to the ground in gasping mirth. He sits on the bed and shakes his head. Your landlady will be up any moment, he says, and then you'll be in for it.

But you're such a good dancer, Inge says. I'd never have believed it.

And you, says Set, pouring two more glasses of whisky, you are the lousiest dancer I've ever taken the floor with.

Inge snorts. It's these huge feet, she says. They're like great bloody bricks! What can I do with them but fall all about the place? She begins unlacing her boots. Set, slightly more sober, kneels to help her. She grabs his wrist. Don't think, she tells him, that I'm undressing for you. She is solemn, holds his eyes; her hair is a bright halo over her round Madonna's face. Then a smile splits it in two, ruins the effect. She purrs with laughter and flings herself onto him.

You're part animal, he says, just after. You're a wild creature. He leaves through the window, climbing down to the porch from the second floor. She watches him go. He waves merrily from the street and jumps in his car, no doubt off to meet Lana for a late dinner. She can tell it costs him nothing to leave, and she wonders if she is the stupidest person alive for giving herself away like this. Is he really a ghost, she wonders, or just a cad with a convenient excuse? But she has also watched him sleep, and she has seen the way his face goes blank and smooth, the way his eyes go so unfo-cused. It seems much too easy for him to slip out of life, Set. She worries that one day he'll forget to slip back in.

＊

Since the bear, Set has always been nervous around large ani-mals on his expeditions. Even the ponies worry him. Their teeth are so big and they give off such an obvious odor; he isn't used to anything that smells and makes no attempt to mask it. And everything smells here in the jungle. The heat creates aggression, even in the smells themselves. They attack, they twist round one and squeeze, insidious, like the vines and other creeping things.

Inge laughs when he tells her this. She has grown up around animals. Horses, dogs, sheep, pigs—their musty earthiness min-gling with the smell of fat sizzling in the kitchen, with the heavy smell of the hanging damp in the walls, the sharp wet of the dung in the hay, the sweet heather on the heath and the dark smoke of wood on the fire.

Odor is geography, she says. And it's the same in the city—but not natural smells, not such animal smells. More people, more soot, more smoke, more smells that get into the lungs and burn the eyes and the throat.

We never lived that way, says Set.

Of course you didn't, she tells him. Your people are wealthy.

Set knows this is true. He feels it is unfair of Inge to be con-stantly pointing it out, when her people were wealthy once, too. Just because they squandered it didn't mean she could cast it off like a dirty old coat. It followed her around the world, the sweet, decayed smell of the genteel poor. Like the dried flowers Pru put in clothing drawers.

But I'm not like that at all, says Inge. Why can't I cast it off?

You just can't, says Set. It clings to you. It makes you careless of the world.

She bristles, but she knows he's right. She remembers when she was very small, and one of her father's friends gave a magic lantern show for the children. This was a few years after her mother died, and her father seemed unlikely to ever pull himself out of his own sadness. And so his friends—back then he still had some—would bring entertainments for his children, puppets and picture books and candies and wooden toys. One particular friend possessed a magic lantern. He was an enormous old banker with a bushy red beard and a huge, booming voice. Inge had been quite afraid of him, until he transformed the walls of the nursery into the walls of the wide world instead. It was the first time Inge had seen such pictures of the sea. The hand-painted glass slides dramatized scenes from "The Wreck of the Hesperus"; there were brightly colored slides of dancing sailors singing sea chanteys, and there was a dramatic battle between French and English ships, complete with cannon fire and burning masts, stark orange in relief against the brilliant blue water. Inge fell in love on the spot, and she knew that someday she would seek these vast oceans, and the places beyond them.

But she thinks now of the feeling of watching the unreal from the safety of one's sleeping quarters. This, she feels sure, is how the world has continued to strike her, through her entire adult life so far. This is a life of watching, observation. Even her camera creates distance. All the more reason she sees to love Set—he may be a ghost, but she's never been more alive, more invested in the world, than when she's with him. She loves him like the sea, and like the sea she'd let him sweep her anywhere.

Set, for his part, wonders if he could be thawing: Is Inge warming him up, or just wearing him down? He is feeling, again, that inevitable pull toward Pru, toward Cedric, toward home. What would happen if he brought Inge with him? Would there be a kind of combustion? Would his soul come crashing back like the end of a spell? He knows he has, at least, to try.

❖

Cedric finally broke his long silence and wrote to Set that fall, a shattering sort of letter. *Great men have passions,* he wrote. *Smaller men are frightened of them. The ruthless seeking of the single-minded—it frightens these small, petty men. They stifle us, smother us, take away our funds. They tell us to branch out, divest. Take up new interests. They call us obsessed. But I'll tell you something: the world needs obsession. No one can blaze a new path in the world without it. All the great explorers had it: Scott, Amundsen, Livingstone, Burton. I should have followed in their footsteps sooner.*

But it's not too late. This find—it's nothing less than the City of the Dead itself. It will be the find of the century—King Tut-ankhamen will be nothing beside it. And you too should leave that terrible place, with its seductions and illusions and fleeting promises of fame, and follow me north to find Hades.

Set was unsure what to make of the letter. He was torn. He owed everything, his life, to Cedric, and yet he frightened Set, seemed too sure he owned his brother's soul. But this was Cedric, *Cedric*—so— should he go? Should he undo the life he'd made in service to his only living brother? What could the past continue to cost?

❖

Back when the War had begun, Inge's German aunt wrote to her of rallies in the street, of crowds spontaneously breaking out into "Die Wacht am Rhein." Inge was disturbed; she loved the works of German playwrights, novelists, and composers. Her aunt sent her Wedekind's *Spring Awakening*, and she read it in a breathless few hours, enthralled. The Germans, far more than her father's people, represented culture for her—they were urbane, artistic, *modern*. And they were her mother's—they were something of her mother's she could hold. Her aunt wrote her that some women in Berlin—including her!—worked in shops, as secretaries, as nurses—in all sorts of professions. The bust of an ancient Egyptian queen named Nefertiti was in display at the Berlin Museum, and Asta Nielsen's films made waves; a woman with a temperament and hair, her aunt said, as wild as Inge's. Even Albert was passionate over German motorcars. Even her father, British to the core, adored Wagner and Strauss.

But then Albert died, and her father tore up the letters as they arrived, pronounced her aunt, and all Germans, spies and murderers. And then the letters eventually stopped coming. And then her aunt disappeared, fled, perhaps, to Switzerland, perhaps to France. Inge missed her voice-on-paper dreadfully.

When her father died, she was not surprised. She and her sisters felt sure, after the War, that he could not last long. He was a man of another era, an Edwardian, looking for fixity, certainty, reliant on tradition. He did not understand the turbulence of this new world—he could not feel safe in such unsteady times. He was too old to find his footing again, especially in a country he didn't belong to, in an Ireland busy uprooting itself, hurling itself forward by violent and unstoppable force.

The men came to their house in the middle of the night. Inge thought it odd they were smashing windows; they could have crawled in through the missing ones in the south wing, or simply walked right in through the door in the kitchen that wouldn't lock. But once her father came to the front door, they were quieter, almost polite. Inge recognized some of them—village boys, one of whom delivered groceries to the house every Wednesday. He kept his hat pulled down, but Inge knew him just the same. And one of them was the cook's boy, who refused to meet her eyes.

The brashest boy shoved Inge aside and demanded the keys from her father. Her father stared, blankly. She wanted to tell the men it was no use, he was already gone. But he finally moved. He went to his office and took up the big ring of keys. He held it out, heavy and jangling, like some foreign body he'd longed to be rid of. They were allowed to pack a small bag, some clothing and a toothbrush and some favorite books, and then they were turned out of doors to watch the fire creeping along, licking the floors, consuming the drapes and the rugs, cracking and tipping the beams until the whole structure collapsed on itself and exploded in a great yellow whoosh.

Inge had never seen anything burn before. She could feel the high heat of the fire from where she stood on the lawn. More villagers had come and were carting away the furniture that hadn't burned up. A small man walked past them with her father's favorite chair slung over his back and called them dirty papists, which she didn't understand at all, because she saw him at the village church each Sunday. She hated the house and had often wished it burnt, or bombed, or otherwise destroyed. And now that it was she didn't feel sorry, exactly, although she was sad, and that was complicated, too. She wished she could have saved the library. That was the hardest hurt of all.

Hannah and Clara were crying—loudly enough that Inge could hear them over the fire. She was almost embarrassed to see them so frightened. It seemed obscene to watch someone's naked fear, and so instead she turned her eyes toward the fire, waited for the last flames to fall, and flicker, and go out.

And in the end, all her father could do was try to save his daughters, to throw them to the mercy of the waters and bow quietly out of the chaos, duty done. He left a note on the blackened floor, next to his last glass of whisky. A quote, from Yeats: "There is no longer a virtuous nation, and the best of us live by candle light." It fluttered away during the shotgun blast, and a gust of wind through the burned parts of roof blew it up and out to sea.

❖

Curiosity #1039: Illuminated manuscript, 180 x 125 mm, circa 1390, titled The Book of the Saints. *Illuminated by The Master of Death—possibly Pierre Remiet.*

❖

Pru has welcomed them as warmly as she knows how. She has made the tea herself and served it in the green and garnet parlor, and Inge has had to stifle a laugh—drinking tea with this old-fashioned matron in a button-neck frock dating back probably to the gay nineties, while strains of fractured jazz spill out of the radio, the orchestra tuning up. Fragments of the past lined up in great cabinets along the wall. Set seems oblivious to the incongruity—though, Inge is quickly discovering, Set seems oblivious to almost anything his strange family does. He seems to think the strangeness is in himself instead. Inge is not sure how they have managed this, his family, but she thinks it is a mean trick.

And here the real strangeness stands now, in Cedric. He stands beside Pru, holds half of a beautiful ivory mask. He wears a necklace of bone. He carries a knife of flint. One of the cabinets is open, its contents spilled onto the parlor rug. Arrowheads and beads and bowstrings. On meeting Inge, he shakes his head sadly and quotes Dante, "These have no hope of death . . . mercy and justice disdain them." So, she thinks, Set's living brother is mad.

Set looks to Pru, shocked, and she shrugs. He's been here for months, she says, but I didn't want to tell you. How could I?

But what about the expedition? Point Hope? Set stares at Cedric, a dark sort of fear frothing up in his hollow place.

Look around you, boy, says Cedric. The city is everywhere— we are uncovering it now, always, forever digging it up. We are always digging up the dead.

Oh, there *is* no city, sighs Pru. There never was. You should have known that. She fingers the buttons on her collar with an unsteady hand. And you should never have brought her into it, she says, and nods at Inge.

Cedric grins at Set, an empty chasm-yawn more grimace than pleasure. Oliver, he says, now he wanted to collect you, that's why he didn't mind what we'd made you. It was only I who suffered, only I who knew what you'd become. He sinks into a chair, seems to shrink into his own skin. You were Oliver's curiosity, he says, but you were always my ghost.

Inge stares at Cedric. Stop telling him insane things, she says. If he's empty inside it's your fault, not his.

Don't you think I don't know that? asks Cedric. He takes off the mask, dashes it to the floor. I've lived every day with that guilt. You can't come back, not truly. There's always a price to be paid by someone. I'm paying for it now.

Set gently pushes Inge aside. Cedric watches them both, Set with a look on his face that he's never seen before, something so open, so willing, that he finds it almost obscene. And the girl— wearing a worshipful gaze like a commedia mask, as frankly and sadly smitten as Pierrot. Something in Cedric springs up in rage, as if he were looking at an abomination he'd created—something so wrong with the fabric of the world that it has to be ripped out. His fault, after all. He couldn't find a dead city; he couldn't find a way back from death. Only one way to fix it now.

Cedric raises the flint knife. Set sees it coming, has always seen it coming, ever since the swimming pool he's seen it, even when he tries not to. And now his brother stabs, rather theatrically, toward him. A gesture, perhaps, but still dangerous. Set twists away but not quite fast enough to avoid a slashed hand. There is a lot of blood, on the carpets, on the wallpaper, on his tan suit. There is blood on Inge's pale cheek. No one speaks. Pru grabs for the knife, but Cedric drops it, already drained of whatever momentary frenzy has possessed him. *Yes sir, that's my baby,* the radio warbles. *No sir, I don't mean maybe.* The clock clicks loudly over the hearth. Even now, time refuses to stand still. Pru kneels next to Cedric, and Inge wonders what on earth Set ever thought she could do for him here. What this place could ever do besides draw life out of a person? This dark house, dead for years? It reminds her so much of her own childhood home, of memories and mourning and halls where the dead stalk the living. It, too, is full of rot.

Set is crying, and she looks for something to bandage his

hand. He shakes his head, and there is nothing ghostly about him now, a mess of earthly blood and tears.

He tried before, he tells Inge. He doesn't know quite what to say, really. What do you say about someone who's saved and destroyed you, over and over again? How do you appease them? How do you live with yourself?

Cedric is quite mad, says Inge. We need to go, Set. We need to leave this place.

This place, says Set. It was Oliver's, too. He stops then, just for a moment. Stops breathing, stops moving, stops his heart. Oliver's. Still there is Oliver here, in the cabinets, the carpets, the stuffed owls and lyres and the lonely fireplace, unlit since he went down to Hades. Set's eyes close. He can almost see it, Oliver's shade in the darkness below, waiting for him. Waiting for his understanding.

Then Set thaws, grabs her hand. Come on, he says, drags her up the little round staircase to his childhood bedroom. There is something he needs to find.

As a small boy, Set wanted to be like Oliver, gentlest of all his siblings. So he started creating his own cabinet, making his own collections. Rocks, sticks, bird feathers, newspaper ads, kazoos and other plastic toys and trinkets, old coins, jacks, ribbons, smooth stones for skipping: he wrapped them each in rags and carefully stuffed them inside of labeled shoeboxes. He had shoeboxes, too, full of intangibles—these, he would have told you, came directly from his head and needed only the reminder of a physical space for storage. Empty boxes lined his bedroom floor, labeled "Clouds" and "Deserts" and "Dreams" inked in neat rounded letters. His siblings gently mocked the empty boxes, all but Oliver. When Oliver saw them, he smiled and said, Where is the one for spirits?

Now Set digs through the wardrobe, pulling out box after box and scattering leaves and rocks and animal bits across the floor.

Set, says Inge. You're bleeding all over. What are you *doing*?

Something I have to find, he says, and dumps out a box labeled "Stamps," another labeled "Butterflies." Bright paper-thin wing parts flutter to the floor. Where is it? Finally he fishes out a box with a different script, smooth and elegant and spelling "Spirits" on the side. Here, he says. He lifts the lid and then his face falls, his shoulders fall, he sits, childhood trinkets sprinkled over the floor like some kind of failed spell. Inge seizes the opportunity to steal a shirt from the wardrobe. She winds it round his bloody hand while he stares into the empty shoebox. She asks what he was expecting to find.

I don't know, he says. Something of Oliver. A message. Something left behind.

Inge wipes the blood from his arm, rolls up his soaking sleeve gently. She has never seen him look so human, so present. She thinks of the burning manor in Larne, of the flames reflected in the face of her father. We all leave something behind, she says.

Downstairs, Cedric is slumped on the rug, staring, surrounded by ruins. Pru has both skinny arms around him. Set loves and hates them both so much in this moment. Inge wonders wildly if Set will disappear when he crosses the threshold, turn to air or salt or sand. Are they all mad here, or is there magic after all?

What was it Constance said? No flying back to the past? Not for Cedric, not for him, not for Inge, not for Pru, not for poor dead Oliver. No second chances.

I won't send him away, says Pru, and Set nods. Of course not, he says.

Inge looks at the two of them, Pru and Cedric, in the dark

surrounded by these dead things in cases. They look like a wax tableau. They look like something in a museum, something fallen from and frozen into the past.

It is 1925, and no one has yet seen the world from above: that vast, comforting blue sphere, softly lit by the sun. But Inge wonders what it must look like to a god, telescoping with such a wide lens. Plunging into the blue of the earth's atmosphere like a high diver, watching the land and water separate, watching the blur spread and shift and become trees, mountains, roads, deserts, houses. Hurtling into the artificial stars of a city, hurtling past brick and glass and concrete and down chimneys and into the hearts of a fractured family. She watches them for a moment, lit by their own strange love, and she wonders what it would be like to feel so strongly about anything you didn't get to choose. She thinks of Albert and then she knows, of course she knows, her heart is bright and heavy with the knowing.

Then, she and Set turn their backs, their heels grinding shards of flint and smears of blood into the green and garnet rug. Are they leaving? Will they be happy? Is anyone ever enough for the person they love?

In the telling, it is always the same. In the telling, the lovers are mired in the past, or moored in the present. In the telling, the bear is always beautiful, the moon is always full above the burning manor, and there are never enough endings.

The Sleepers

Ancient dreams cling like crumbs to the mouths of the sleepers. They mutter and twitch, chasing after phantom women, fragments of words, half-drunk goblets of wine. This is what the sleepers find outside of history: a weakness in repose for which there is no cure but dreaming. The dreams of men become akin to the dreams of all creatures, the dreams of dogs and horses and goats and pigs, rooting in the muck of the past and the possible. A sleep not death, but something close—a sleep like wishing for life.

Since the first sleep of Cronus, countless sleepers have pulled the centuries over them like blankets. Frederick Barbarossa under the Kyffhäuser hills; Owain Glyndŵr in a secret corner of Wales; St. Wenceslas and his knights in Blaník Mountain; the Golem in the Old New Synagogue in Prague; Bernardo Carpio in the caves of Montelban; Bran the Blessed under the White Hill, facing France; Montezuma in the mountain; Charlemagne in the Untersberg; Merlin in the oak tree; and of course Arthur, alone in Craig-y-Ddinas, or with the three ladies in Avalon, or among the Eildons in Roxburghshire, or with his men among the stars.

These dreams are rarely restful. The men who dream them knew nothing of rest when awake. Their lives were mad and glorious and they were pure motion, streaks of flame burning through their own eras, their brilliance blurring all down the centuries except for the fact that there was brilliance, there is brilliance still, lying dormant and deep under the dreams. For gold, yes. For love, yes. For lust, yes, for blood, for glory, for power, for country, for freedom, and sometimes just for the sheer dear pleasure of the fight, the fortune won or lost or defended.

They are many, even in dreams more than most, their names tucked into the hills and tilled with the soil of the ages. Only the oldest stones remember their faces; only the tallest trees still look upon their figures. Their deaths could not be borne and so would never be; instead they folded themselves into a sleep as long and deep as legend. They became legend, their names dust in the mouths of their enemies. They became hope splashed across the stricken brows of their people, drunk greedily when all other waters had dried up.

Buried deep in mountains or under the earth or in our oldest dwellings, they wound their way into ballad and verse. They began to appear in visions, dreamer and dreamed tied by the long taut rope woven through myth and prophecy. You are coming, the seers would tell them, down the centuries you will ride until at last you reach us. You are coming to save us, they would say. And the sleepers would nod, and sleep on, and sleep on.

They are now forgotten mostly, remembered in dreams and stories, through poems and song. They want to be forgotten, they *need* to be forgotten—for the consequences of waking have grown too great.

Shut up so long in the same earth and rock, their stories begin to bleed together. They confuse themselves with their own chroniclers.

And so, like Taliesin, they trundle out wild tales sprawling across the centuries and spanning many lands. The sleepers were mighty once, but now they have fallen into half-life; they are suits of armor stored in mothballs, cheated out of their final hours of glory. They linger in tragic, hopeful limbo and smell of ancient halls, of savage times and violent spirits, brought down by time and by the telling of their tales.

Those who were made to take action will sleep for all time. They will sleep, because to wake is to quicken, to be roused and alert and alive. They will not wake, not yet, not ever, because with their waking comes the death of all dreams, the snuffing of all those flares in the darkness, the crumble and fall of those towers where men still wait for the sleepers to save them. Awake too late, in a sleep-deprived time, we dream but foolishly of heroes. We dream in vain, for with their waking comes the end of the hope of the world.

Acknowledgments

Thank yous are terrible for the polite Midwesterner, because one cannot possibly thank all of the people who deserve it—for the great gifts of time and advice and support and love needed to make art. Nonetheless, plunging right in: thank you to the first readers of much of this book. Matt Bell, Steve Himmer, Erin Fitzgerald, Robert Kloss—you have immeasurably improved these words with your much-needed advice and wise writers' eyes, and I am so damned grateful for your friendship. Thank you to Karissa Kloss for being one half of the best team ever, Team Kloss, and being such a stellar supporter of the writers in her life. Thank you to Jacob, Victor, Ben, Lauren, and the team at Curbside Splendor for the early support and encouragement. Thank you to those who published many of the pieces in this book, giving them a first home: Nate Brown, Gabriel Blackwell, Lincoln Michel, Matt Bell, Randall Brown, Blake Butler, Jamie Iredell, Dave Housley, Roxane Gay, Joey Pizzolato, and Erik Smetana. Thank you to Mark Cugini and Laura Spencer for helping to create a real, welcoming literary community here in D.C. Thank you to the team at Liveright, and especially to my amazingwonderfulfabulous editor Katie Adams for believing in this book and making it a better book, the best it could be—and also for the excellent new parent advice. Thank you to Kent Wolf for being the kind of passionate advocate for my words that I dreamed of in an agent, and for having the best hair, hands down. Thank you to my mom and dad, as always, because without them there are no stories. And thank you, especially, to Christopher Backley, without whom the world would truly be unfinished for me.